ADVENTURE ISLAND

THE MYSTERY
OF THE BLACK SALAMANDER

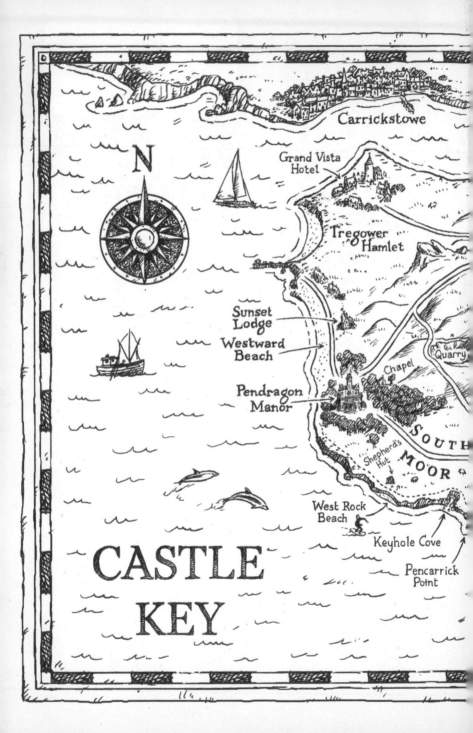

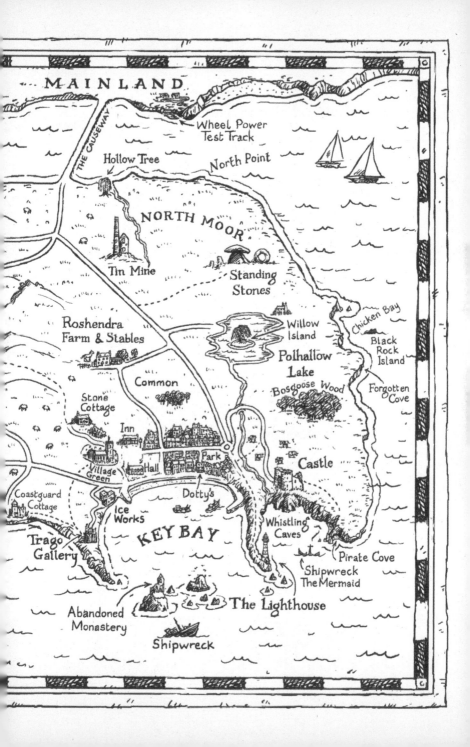

Collect all the Adventure Island *books*

ADVENTURE ISLAND

THE MYSTERY OF THE BLACK SALAMANDER

Helen Moss

Illustrated by Leo Hartas

Orion
Children's Books

ORION CHILDREN'S BOOKS

First published in Great Britain in 2013 by Orion Children's Books
This edition published in 2017 by Hodder and Stoughton

5 7 9 10 8 6

A CIP catalogue record for this book
is available from the British Library.

ISBN 978 1 4440 0756 5

Printed and bound in Great Britain
by Clays Ltd, St Ives plc

The paper and board used in this book are
made from wood from responsible sources.

Orion Children's Books
An imprint of
Hachette Children's Group
Part of Hodder and Stoughton
Carmelite House
50 Victoria Embankment
London EC4Y 0DZ

An Hachette UK Company
www.hachette.co.uk

www.hachettechildrens.co.uk

For Sam and Tom

One

Exciting News

It was a high-risk mission but Jack Carter knew he could handle it. He had a priceless cargo to deliver. And he had to move fast. The payload was extremely unstable. In this heat, total meltdown could happen at any second.

Sweat ran into his eyes. Jack blinked it away. He gauged the distance to the exit. His knuckles tightened as he gripped the tray. He turned from the counter and struck out across no man's land, the James Bond theme playing in his head. A tricky little backward shimmy through the door in the slipstream of a departing customer and he was out.

Mission accomplished!

'One strawberry sundae,' he said, handing a tall glass of ice cream to his brother, who was sitting in the shade of a striped parasol, squinting at his iPod screen.

'And, for me, choco-banoffee-marshmallow-cookie-dough ice cream with extra whipped cream, rainbow sprinkles and caramel sauce.' Jack stood back to admire the spectacular creation.

Scott pulled a face. 'That looks gross!'

Jack frowned. 'You're right! It's definitely missing something.' He headed back into Dotty's Tea Rooms. A moment later he emerged from the café and placed a shiny red cherry on the top. 'There! A work of art!'

It was one of those hot, sticky days when the sky bulged with purple clouds, and little black thunderbugs flew into your hair and – for reasons known only to themselves – tried to crawl up your nose. Jack and Scott had spent the morning helping Aunt Kate in the garden at Stone Cottage. Ever since their first visit to Castle Key last summer, when they'd met Emily Wild and solved the mystery of the whistling caves, they'd come to stay with their aunt – technically their *great*-aunt – every school holiday, while their dad was off travelling the world on archaeological digs. Their mum had died in a car accident when Jack was so little that he wasn't sure whether his memories of her were real, or whether he was just remembering the faded photos in the old albums.

Looking up from his ice cream Jack saw Emily bombing along the seafront on her bike. She was standing up on the pedals, her long brown curls streaming out behind her. She skidded to a halt, her front tyre bumping the edge of the table. Drift hopped down from his special basket on the back, wagging his tail in bliss. After his beloved Emily, Jack and Scott were his all-time favourite humans. *And* they had ice cream!

'Exciting news ...' Emily panted. 'I've just heard ...'

Jack and Scott exchanged grins. Knowing Emily, she'd uncovered a smuggling ring, a treasure map or, at the very least, a plot to steal the Crown Jewels.

'... from the Castle Key Nature Watch Group!' Emily went on.

Nature Group? A lump of ice cream slithered down Jack's gullet. He hadn't felt this disappointed since his last birthday present from Gran turned out to be a pair of socks. He wouldn't have minded so much, but they'd been pink with ballerinas all over them.

Jack had nothing against nature. He liked animals. He loved Drift, of course, and Aunt Kate's tabby kitten, Boomerang. And during their last case he'd even been appointed by the Carrickstowe Police as official guardian to the Prince of Medania's white mouse (long story!). But as far as Jack was concerned, nature didn't like *him*; it was always biting him, stinging him or crawling up his nose. He was sure a couple of those thunderbugs were still camping out inside his right nostril. *And don't even get me started on spiders*, he thought.

Emily helped herself to a spoonful of Jack's ice cream. 'We're talking *killer whales*!' she said dramatically.

Suddenly Jack was interested. Killer whales were *serious* wildlife, like tigers and polar bears: the kind of nature you saw on TV programmes.

'I didn't know there were orcas in Cornwall,' Scott said.

Jack snorted – not a wise move with a nose full of thunderbugs and a mouthful of ice cream. *Typical of Scott 'Know-it-All' Carter to show off by using the scientific name*, he thought.

'It's very rare to see them here,' Emily agreed, 'but two were spotted off North Point this morning. You guys coming to see?'

—

The friends cycled out of Castle Key village, over the common and along the track across North Moor. It was a wild and remote corner of the island. A few sheep meandered among clumps of gorse and heather cropping the short, springy grass. Seagulls wailed high overhead. The only signs that humans had ever passed this way were the abandoned tin mine and the ancient standing stones.

But that all changed when they reached the coast. A small crowd had gathered on North Point, a craggy promontory where huge boulders were stacked in tumbling heaps and strewn around like giant Jenga blocks.

Everyone was staring out across the water. Some had obviously settled in for the day, with folding chairs and flasks of tea. Emily took the binoculars from the investigation kit she always carried in her shoulder bag. She looked for a moment, shook her head and handed them to Jack. He scanned the sea for a pair of jet-black dorsal fins knifing through the water. He could see fishing boats and seagulls, and the buildings on the mainland a mile or so across the channel, but not a single fin.

A man with a disorganized sandy beard and sideburns and a clipboard pressed to his *Save the Rainforest* t-shirt broke away from the crowd. 'Super! Super! Some new young members for the Nature Watch Group. That's what I like to see.' He shook hands all round and introduced himself as Don Penrose. 'We think a mother and a calf must have strayed from their pod and got lost.'

'Maybe they've swum back out to sea,' Scott said. 'Don't they have to come up to breathe every few minutes?'

Don Penrose nodded. 'That's right. We'll keep watching in case they haven't found their way out of the channel.' He thrust his clipboard at the friends. 'Great to have you on board!' Before they knew what was happening, they'd all filled out application forms and signed up to the Castle Key Nature Watch Group.

'Super! I'll put you three down for the early watch on Wednesday, shall I?' Penrose enthused as he handed them each a member's badge. 'Report at six a.m. sharp.'

As they left, Jack shook his head in disbelief. Had he really just joined a nature group? As he picked up his bike he felt something plop on his head. Great! A welcome message from a low-flying seagull!

They were halfway across North Moor when he felt another plop. Then another. But this time it wasn't gulls. There was a rumble of thunder. Diagonal rain came sweeping across the moors and most of it seemed to find its way down the back of Jack's t-shirt.

'Nature!' he groaned. 'Don't you just love it!'

—

Next morning, Scott was woken by the *Match of the Day* ringtone on his phone. He peered at the screen. 'It's Emily!' he muttered.

'Tell me it's not another urgent communication from the Nature Watch Group,' Jack grumbled from under his quilt on the other side of the cosy attic bedroom. 'What is it this time? A herd of invisible rhinos stampeding across the common?'

Scott had the phone to his ear now. 'She says do we want to go and see the black salamander ...'

'*Salamander*? Isn't that some kind of lizard?' Jack said. 'I think I'll pass.'

But Scott was pushing himself up on his elbows. 'She's talking about *the* Black Salamander!'

Jack sat up so fast he cracked his head on the sloping ceiling. 'No way! That awesome new supercar they were talking about on *Top Gear* the other day? The one with bazillions of cool gadgets? The one that can dive underwater like a submarine?'

Scott could hardly speak for excitement.

He didn't need to.

A single nod of the head said it all!

Two

The Coolest Car on the Planet

As they jumped on their bikes, one super-sized question kept whizzing round Scott's head: how had Emily wangled the chance to see the world's most talked-about supercar? The Black Salamander was so exclusive that only one prototype had been built. The car magazines and websites had been buzzing with rumours about it for months.

'I had a call from Max Fordham this morning,'

Emily explained, as the boys pulled up to meet her on the high street. 'You remember – from Operation Lost Star?'

Scott and Jack both nodded. Max wasn't the kind of guy you forgot in a hurry. He was an ex-SAS soldier who now worked as a stunt co-ordinator for the film industry. Last summer he'd come to stay at The Lighthouse in Castle Key – which Emily's parents ran as a Bed and Breakfast – while working on location on a movie. When Savannah Shaw, the star of the film, had gone missing, Emily, Jack, Scott and Drift were soon on the case.

'The Black Salamander is going to feature in this new Hollywood movie called *Ocean Force*,' Emily went on. 'Max is designing all the stunts, so he's come to see the car in action at the Wheel Power test track.'

'Wow!' Jack whistled. 'That's just outside Carrickstowe, isn't it? What are we waiting for?'

The Wheel Power test track was on the site of an old airbase not far from the causeway that crossed the narrow channel from Castle Key island. The friends gazed up at the huge metal gates. High-security mesh fencing was festooned with razor wire and bristled with cameras.

Emily stood on tiptoe to reach the speakerphone and

asked nervously for Max Fordham. The gates creaked open. Feeling very small, she and the boys pushed their bikes into a large compound. The gates clanged shut behind them.

Max strolled out from an ugly, red brick building that looked like part of an old Victorian hospital. With his black t-shirt and combat trousers, he looked as if he might still be on special operations with the army, but his steely blue eyes crinkled as he raised his hands for high-fives all round.

'Do we have a problem, Max?'

They all turned to see a slim woman in a red spotted dress hurrying towards them on skyscraper heels. Her glossy black hair glowed with coppery highlights in the bright sunshine. She spoke with an American accent.

'Not at all,' Max answered. 'Scott, Jack and Emily are friends of mine. I've invited them to see the Salamander.'

The woman pursed her red-glossed lips for a moment, then flashed a dazzling smile. 'I am so loving this,' she said. 'Engaging with young people in the community. That *always* plays well.' She nodded as if agreeing with herself. 'I know! We'll do a photo-shoot with the Salamander.' She looked the friends up and down as if they were dresses in the end-of-season sale. 'Hmm, a pretty face, but we'll need a hairbrush...' she murmured to Emily. She smiled at Scott. 'Fabulous. Loving that floppy-haired boy band look.' Then she came to Jack, slowly taking in the sticking-up hair, the ketchup-stained t-shirt and the grubby knees. Her smile wobbled, but only for a second. 'Nothing we can't sort out in Photoshop!' With that, she whipped a phone out of her handbag and dashed away, reeling off instructions as she went.

'*Boy band!*' Scott snorted, although he couldn't help a blush creeping over his ears.

'*Hairbrush!*' Emily fumed.

'*Photoshop!*' Jack spluttered.

Max laughed. 'That was Alesha Rahal. She's in charge of publicity for Silverwood Motors – that's the company that makes the Black Salamander. She's quite harmless, just a bit ...'

'Bonkers?' Jack suggested.

'I was going to say *full-on!*'

'Publicity?' Scott asked. 'I thought the Black Salamander was all hush-hush?'

'It has been so far,' Max said. 'Silverwood had to make sure other car companies couldn't copy the design or steal all their cutting-edge technology before it was finished. But now the Salamander is almost ready to roll and they can start showing her off. After the last few performance tests here she'll be whisked off to the Monaco Motor Show to be unveiled in a blaze of glory – then shipped to Hollywood to start filming.'

Max tapped a code into the security pad on the door of the red brick building and ushered the friends inside.

They signed their names at a reception desk and were given visitor passes to hang round their necks. Then they walked out through the other side of the building, past storerooms, garages and workshops, until they came to a racing circuit in the shape of a figure of eight. It was cordoned off with crash barriers and stacks of tyres. Cones and chicanes had been set out along one side of the track.

'Silverwood Motors are based near Birmingham, aren't they?' Scott asked Max, as they leaned on a barrier and watched a red Ferrari and a silver Lamborghini zoom onto the track. 'Why have they brought the Salamander all the way to Cornwall for testing?'

Max shaded his eyes against the sun. 'It's because they can test all the underwater functions here as well as the road performance. There's an artificial lake over there.' He pointed to a stretch of water beyond the track. A powerboat was speeding along in a plume of spray. 'And at the back of the compound,' Max continued, 'there's a private harbour where they can test the car in seawater ...'

Max's words were drowned out as the Ferrari and the Lamborghini roared past. *It's a good thing we left Drift at home*, Jack thought. That noise would have blown a fuse in his hypersensitive ears! Jack, on the other hand, loved it – the sound throbbed through muscle and bone to his very core. And the smell! He breathed in petrol fumes, burning rubber and oil. *Heaven*!

Now a third car had appeared on the circuit. Unlike the other two, it hardly made a sound, even though it was travelling at phenomenal speed. The air shimmered around it in a heat haze.

As the car whispered to a stop in front of them Jack let out a long sigh of awe. It sat low and wide and sleek, its black paintwork glistening in the sunshine, as slick as if it were wet. Air vents along the flanks gave it the menace of a shark. Jack grinned at Scott and nodded. The Black Salamander had *everything*: the raw power of a Bugatti Veyron, the style of an Aston Martin and the silent speed of a stealth bomber.

The doors opened upwards like the outstretched wings of a giant bat. For a moment Jack expected Batman himself to spring out, cape aflutter. Instead a tall man in white overalls eased out of the cockpit. He pulled off his helmet and raked a hand through his sun-streaked hair.

'This is Connor Jamison,' Max said. 'The Black Salamander's official driver.'

Jack had to stop himself bowing down in worship. Connor Jamison was only the sharpest new British Formula One driver since Lewis Hamilton!

Max clapped the driver on the shoulder. 'Connor is going to be the stunt double for the lead actor in Ocean Force. And I've got some immense stunts lined up for him!'

Connor Jamison grinned. 'I get to do all the dangerous stuff! Cool, eh?'

Just then a mechanic hurried over from one of the workshops to tell Connor that the new oil filters he'd asked about were ready. Scott and Jack listened happily as Connor discussed intercoolers and twin turbos.

Emily tuned out. She wasn't interested in engines. She just wanted to find out about the gadgets and the going-underwater part. As she gazed around she spotted Alesha Rahal hurrying towards them. A man in black jeans and t-shirt loped along at her side. His designer stubble and sunglasses gave him a cool-without-even-trying look, and a bulky camera bobbed on his chest with each step. Emily guessed he must be a reporter. Alesha was holding her phone to her ear. And what was that in her other hand? Not ... a *hairbrush*!

Emily dived behind the Black Salamander. No one was coming near her hair with a brush! Even her mum had given up years ago! She peeked out and saw Alesha introducing the reporter to Scott and Jack. 'This is Shane Hazard, from *Motor Mania* magazine. We thought *Ace driver shows off supercar to local kids* would make a nice little feature.' She waved the hairbrush in Scott's direction. 'Now, where's your friend? A pretty face will widen the market appeal.'

Emily had almost crawled underneath the Salamander now. She could feel the heat radiating from the black metal. A little red light winked under the exhaust pipe.

Suddenly she heard a voice behind her. She looked round, preparing to dodge the hairbrush, but the voice belonged to a young man in a leather jacket who was sitting on a stack of tyres.

'Yeah,' he muttered into his phone. 'Connor Jamison is swanning around playing the big hero again ...'

The man paused and looked to the side. Emily realized with a start that his ginger hair hadn't been deliberately shaved into a punk style, as she'd thought at first, but was growing in patchy tufts. His forehead and scalp were horribly scarred down one side, the skin waxy and warped like a melted candle. 'Just because Jamison's got the film-star looks,' he continued, 'Silverwood fob me off with "back-up driver" and *he* gets Monaco and Hollywood!' He listened for a moment. Then he laughed softly. 'I know! Tonight's the night. Don't worry, I'll be there ...'

Meanwhile, on the other side of the Black Salamander, Connor Jamison looked at his watch. 'We need to crack on with the underwater testing in a minute.' He turned to Shane Hazard. 'Do you want to get a couple of quick shots of the boys sitting in the car first?'

Shane Hazard gave a thumbs-up. 'Sounds good.'

Jack couldn't believe his luck! He was going to get his photograph in *Motor Mania* magazine with the coolest car on the planet! His friends back in London were going to be so jealous! Surely any minute now his alarm clock would go off and he'd wake up to find this was all a dream. He reached out towards the Salamander just to check it was real.

Wee-wah! Wee-wah! Wee-wah!

Jack shot back and clapped his hands over his ears. The noise blared louder than a *million* alarm clocks! Security alarms were going off all over the compound.

Three

Security Alert

'I didn't touch it!' Jack yelped.

'Nor me!' Emily cried, popping up from behind the Black Salamander.

Max was glancing rapidly from side to side like a soldier under enemy fire. 'Someone must have tried to break in.'

'Initiate lock-down procedure!' voices shouted all over the compound. Security guards ran back and forth.

Metal shutters slammed down over the workshops and garages.

Connor jumped back into the cockpit. 'I'll lock the Salamander into the top-security garage ...' But before he could start the engine the alarms stopped wailing and a security guard jogged over to join them.

'Panic over,' the guard puffed. 'It was just Frank.' He jerked his thumb towards a forklift truck crawling across the compound. 'He popped out to pick up a delivery and mistyped his code into the keypad when he came back in.'

The forklift driver – a middle-aged man with a jowly face that gave him the look of a friendly bulldog – leaned out of the cab as he passed and slapped his forehead. 'Sorry! I'd forget my own head if it wasn't screwed on!'

The security guard rolled his eyes. 'Second time that's happened this week,' he grumbled. 'Well, I'm on the nightshift tonight as well! I need a coffee!' With that he stomped off in the direction of a grey Portakabin building that looked to Jack just like the temporary classrooms that dotted his school.

Alesha Rahal smiled as if she'd planned the whole event. 'As you can see, security is top-notch here.' She looked up as a man with a bald head encircled by a monk-like fringe of white hair came to join them.

'This is Monty Howard,' Max told the friends. 'Chief engineer at Silverwood Cars – the brains behind the Black Salamander. The Salamander has its own built-in security systems too, doesn't it, Monty?' he added.

Monty Howard leaned on his walking stick, took a handkerchief from the pocket of his corduroy jacket and polished his glasses. 'Oh, yes,' he chuckled. 'There are two GPS trackers behind the dashboard. If anyone tries to steal the car, the trackers send signals back to head office to tell us exactly where it is.' He gazed fondly at the Salamander, like a grandfather beaming at a favourite grandchild. He tapped the side of his nose. 'And just this morning I decided to install a third, top-secret GPS device. I've not told anyone where it's hidden.' He grinned and patted Connor Jamison's arm. 'Not even our driver here! So even if the other two trackers were removed, we'd still be able to pinpoint the car's exact location.' He turned to Scott, Jack and Emily. 'Now, I bet you'd like to see some of the Salamander's more *unusual* features.'

At last, Emily thought, *we get to see the gadgets!*

Connor Jamison grimaced. 'Don't be too long. Otherwise we'll miss our testing slot at the lake.'

Monty Howard nodded. He clearly loved showing off his invention. 'Yes, of course.' He handed his walking stick to Scott and slid into the cockpit. He demonstrated the passenger-side ejector seat (launching a crash-test dummy into orbit), the air tanks for breathing underwater, the infrared cameras, periscope and radio communication devices. 'And then there's this!' he said, twiddling a dial. 'Stand back!'

Scott, Emily and Jack waited excitedly, but nothing happened. They exchanged puzzled looks.

Then suddenly the car disappeared.

'Wow!' Jack shouted. 'That's magic!'

Scott took a step forwards, gaping at the place where the Black Salamander had stood just the moment before. He could detect a slight shimmer. 'Not magic,' he laughed. 'It's active camouflage! I've read about it but I never thought it would be *that* good!'

Suddenly the Salamander reappeared, as black and shiny as ever. Monty opened the door and grinned up at them. 'Computer-generated images that match the background are projected onto the sides of the car so that it blends in perfectly. So far it only really works when the car is standing still, but we're getting there!'

'It's just like a chameleon!' Emily breathed.

Monty Howard smiled. 'A lot of the best ideas for new technology come from the world of nature.'

Jack wasn't convinced. Since when did *nature* have widescreen TV or microwave popcorn? But he didn't argue.

'You know why I named this car the Black Salamander?' Monty asked.

'Er, because it's *black*?' Jack ventured.

Scott rolled his eyes. 'Salamanders are amphibians.

They can live in the water as well as on land. Like a frog or a newt.'

Jack grinned at Monty. 'I'm glad you didn't call it the Black Newt. It just doesn't have the same ring to it!'

'Quite!' Monty chuckled. 'But there's another reason I chose the name. Do you know the legend of the fire salamander?'

'Is it a new X-Men film?' Jack asked.

Monty shook his head. 'Since ancient times people have believed that salamanders lived in fire. That was the inspiration for *this* feature.' He pressed a button on the dashboard. Jets of flame shot out of the front of the car. He pressed another button and a thick black smokescreen billowed out from the back. 'Just like the mythical salamander, this car can withstand very high temperatures,' he explained. 'And there's another myth that says the sticky substance that salamanders secrete when they're attacked is so toxic that if a salamander climbs into an apple tree, all the apples become deadly poisonous. Now, this is my version … stand clear!'

Globs of green gunge spurted out from the back of the car, hitting the ground with loud splats. 'Don't worry,' Monty laughed. 'It's not toxic. Just incredibly sticky. I've planned a great chase scene for the movie where all the other cars get stuck to the road as they cross a drawbridge! The Salamander will just dive off into the river, of course! Which reminds me, we'd better get on with that underwater testing.'

Scott, Jack and Emily arrived at the testing lake just as Connor Jamison drove the Salamander into the water. There was a whirring sound as the wheels retracted and two huge triangular fins flipped up at the back, then the car plunged beneath the surface leaving only a stream of bubbles in its wake.

They watched in fascination as Max, Monty, Connor – and several other engineers and mechanics – put all the car's submarine functions through their paces. As they worked, Monty Howard kept up a running commentary, explaining how the special controls and functions operated. 'The main challenge is the driver's air supply,' he told them. 'It only lasts about twenty minutes at the moment, but we're working on it.'

Eventually Max looked at his watch. 'Who's ready for a pizza?' he offered. 'I have to leave right after lunch to catch a plane to Los Angeles for a meeting with the film directors.'

The friends didn't need to be asked twice!

This is not normal, Scott thought, as he cycled along the high street the following morning.

Normal people were tucked up in bed at twenty to six on a Wednesday morning, not on their way to look for a pair of whales, which were probably cruising around the mid-Atlantic by now – that's if they even *existed*! The sighting was probably someone's idea of a joke! *Do I look like I'm laughing?* Scott asked himself grimly, swerving round a parked car and almost colliding with a man unloading bundles of *The Carrickstowe Times* from the back of a van outside the newsagent.

'Watch out!' the delivery man shouted. 'You alright, mate?' he added. 'You look a bit weird.'

Jack fishtailed to a halt next to Scott. 'Don't worry! My brother always looks weird, especially at this time in the morning!'

Scott was still staring down at the early edition of *The Carrickstowe Times*.

The delivery man peeled a copy off the top of the pile and handed it to Scott. 'Here, take one if you're so interested. I've got some spares.'

Scott mumbled his thanks, his eyes still fixed on the front-page headline.

This was definitely *not* a normal morning.

—

Twenty minutes later Scott and Jack met Emily and Drift on North Point.

Don Penrose, who had been on the night watch, eased up from his deckchair and stretched his stiff legs. 'Still no sign of those orcas,' he sighed. Handing out clipboards, binoculars and a camera, he explained how to record sightings. Then he folded up his chair and headed home.

The friends quickly swept their binoculars across the water. No whales! They noted the time and entered NIL on the grid on the survey sheet. Then they sat down on the rocks to pore over the newspaper. They barely noticed that the rising sun was streaking the sky with salmon pink and tangerine. They had more urgent matters on their minds than sunrises or killer whales.

The Black Salamander had disappeared in the night!

Four

Unbelievable!

Emily stared at the headline.

'HIGH-TECH SUPERCAR STOLEN FROM TOP-SECURITY TEST TRACK,' she read out loud for the fifth time.

'Top security!' Jack spluttered. 'You can say that again! All those code numbers and guards and cameras. You couldn't pinch a custard cream in that place without the alarms going off! How on earth did anyone get out with the Black Salamander?'

'The police say it was loaded onto a lorry,' Scott said, reading to the end of the article. 'They have CCTV camera footage of the truck leaving the Wheel Power test track and heading for the main road. They even know *where* the Salamander was taken – the thieves removed the two GPS trackers and dumped them, but they obviously didn't know about that secret one that Monty Howard added. It tracked the Salamander all the way to Plymouth before the signal cut out.'

Jack tugged the paper out of Scott's hands and read it for himself. 'Well, that figures. Plymouth is a major port, isn't it? It says here that the lorry was seen driving onto one of those big car ferries that go over to Europe.'

Scott nodded. 'Probably stolen to order by an organized crime ring ...' He paused, suddenly noticing that Emily was very quiet. That was a most unusual state of affairs – especially when the conversation involved organized crime rings.

'The Black Salamander could be halfway round the world by now.' Jack puffed out his cheeks and sighed. 'It's unbelievable!'

Emily looked at him with a mysterious expression on her face. 'Exactly!'

'What do you mean, *exactly*?' Scott asked.

'I mean, it *is* unbelievable and I, for one, *don't* believe it.'

Jack gaped at Emily. 'You don't believe the

Salamander's been stolen? What? You think they've just forgotten where they put it?'

Emily laughed. 'Of course I believe it's been stolen. It's the bit about it being carted off to Plymouth on the back of a lorry I'm not buying.'

'But the lorry was caught on camera,' Scott pointed out. 'The secret GPS tracker was sending signals all the way there.'

Emily shook her head. 'It's all too *obvious*!'

Jack grinned at Scott. That was the First Law According to Emily Wild: never believe a simple explanation if you can find another one ten times more complicated. 'What's your theory, then?' he asked.

Emily stood up and scanned the sea with the binoculars. Still no whales. She sat back down and entered another NIL on the survey sheet. 'What if the secret tracker *was* removed from the Salamander?' she said. 'One of the thieves puts the tracker inside the lorry and drives it all the way to Plymouth to make everyone *think* that's where the car has gone. Meanwhile, an accomplice takes the Salamander somewhere completely different where nobody's looking for it!'

Jack shook his head. 'That tracker *can't* have been removed. Monty Howard said he'd only just installed it and he hadn't told anyone where it was located.'

For once Scott agreed with his brother. 'That's right. He hadn't even told Connor Jamison and *he's* the driver!'

But Emily smiled. '*I* know where it was!'

The boys stared at her. 'Yeah, right!' they scoffed in chorus.

Emily ignored them. 'And so might any of the people who were with us at the track yesterday,' she went on. 'When Monty Howard was telling us about the hidden tracking device he kept looking at the back of the car.' She pulled a thick hardback book out of her bag and tapped the cover.

Jack recognized the book straight away. *Lie Detection: Theory and Methods* was some of Emily's favourite reading matter. It had too many words and not enough jokes for Jack's liking, but he had to admit it had saved their skin on more than one occasion.

'When people have hidden something, they can't help looking at their hiding place when they're talking about it,' Emily explained.

'So Monty was looking at the back of the car,' Scott said. 'That's not exactly very specific.'

'The tracker was just under the exhaust pipe. There was this little flashing light. I saw it when I was hiding, I mean, er ...' Emily hesitated, not wanting to bring up the hairbrush episode.

But it was too late. 'Ah, yes, beware the Evil Alesha and her Hairbrush of Doom!' Jack cackled. He grabbed handfuls of his hair and lurched around the rocks making bloodcurdling noises. Drift thought it was a game and joined in, prancing around Jack's feet, yipping excitedly.

Scott laughed. Jack was right. Emily would think nothing of chasing a gang of armed criminals across the moors at midnight, but she had run a mile from that hairbrush!

Emily stuck her tongue out at Jack. 'The point is – if *I* figured out where that tracker was, anyone else who was there could have done, too.'

'You mean it was an inside job?' Jack asked.

Emily nodded.

'Hang on!' Scott said. 'If the Black Salamander *wasn't* in the lorry, how did they drive it out of Wheel Power without being caught on camera?'

'Duh!' Jack laughed. 'They switched on the active camouflage, of course! They made it invisible.'

'That's right!' Emily said. 'Which is another reason we know there's an insider involved – someone who knows how to work the features on the Salamander.'

Scott wasn't convinced. Hadn't Monty told them that the active camouflage only worked properly when the car was standing still? But there was no stopping Emily when she had her teeth into an idea! By the time Scott had done another whale-check and entered NIL on the survey sheet, she'd already taken out her notebook, turned to a new page, written *OPERATION SALAMANDER* and underlined it twice.

Jack reached for his backpack and extracted a silver foil parcel. He'd not had time to finish his breakfast before leaving Stone Cottage. 'It's bad for your health to start an investigation on an empty stomach,' he mumbled through a mouthful of toast and marmalade. 'Everyone knows that!'

Under the heading Emily wrote the word SUSPECTS in capital letters. 'Right!' she said. 'We need a list of all the people who could have heard Monty talking about the secret GPS tracker when we were there yesterday.'

Scott and Jack looked at each other. They still weren't totally convinced by Emily's theory, but they had to start somewhere. And it wasn't as if they could go off to Plymouth and start snooping around the ferry terminal. The police would have that covered anyway. 'Connor Jamison was there!' Jack offered.

Emily nodded and wrote down the name of the official driver. 'He'd certainly know how all the gadgets worked on the car too.'

'But why would Connor want to steal the car when he was going to get all that fame and fortune doing the stunt driving for the movie?' Scott pointed out.

Emily chewed the end of her pen. 'We'll worry about motives later.'

'My money's on Alesha Rahal!' Jack laughed. 'She was there. And if she can attack Emily with a hairbrush in cold blood, who knows *what* she's capable of?'

'Not very likely, though, is it?' Scott said. 'The Salamander going missing isn't exactly great publicity for Silverwood Cars!'

Emily added Alesha's name to the list, along with

Shane Hazard, the reporter from *Motor Mania*, and Frank, the forklift driver. He'd been unloading tyres not far away from the Black Salamander. It was possible he'd overheard Monty talking about the secret tracker.

'And there was that mechanic who came over to tell Connor about the oil filters,' Emily added. 'It should be easy enough to find out her name. There can't be many female mechanics working there.'

'She's called Elizabeth Price,' Jack said. 'There was a name label on her overalls.' Jack felt rather proud of himself. Emily had nagged him about improving his observation skills so many times in the past that he'd got in the habit of noticing things just in case she sprang a surprise test on him later.

Emily added Elizabeth Price's name to her list. She also added Monty Howard, although, as Scott pointed out, why he'd want to steal the car he'd invented himself was anyone's guess!

Emily sighed and stared at her list. Six suspects and not a decent motive between them! They could have done it for the money, of course, but it would be almost impossible to find a buyer for a stolen car as easily recognizable as the Black Salamander. Suddenly she remembered someone they'd missed. 'The guy with the scarred face!' she exclaimed. She quickly told Scott and Jack about the man she'd overheard talking on the phone when she'd been dodging Alesha's hairbrush.

'Tufty ginger hair? Scarred face?' Scott repeated.

'That sounds like Will Stone. He was this big up and coming Formula One driver, but he had a massive crash at the Italian Grand Prix a couple of years ago. He was badly burned.'

'Well, he was fed up about Connor Jamison being chosen as the official driver of the Black Salamander,' Emily said. 'Maybe he's the thief.'

Scott nodded slowly. 'It makes sense. Will Stone could have stolen the Black Salamander in revenge for not being picked as the stunt driver.'

Emily and the boys grinned at each other in excitement. At last they had a decent clue to work on!

Five

A Busy Morning

Emily was writing PRIME SUSPECT next to Will Stone's name when she noticed Drift's ears flick into Listening Formation. She glanced up to see two teenaged girls racing over the rocks towards them. Emily recognized Vicky White, who lived at Roshendra Farm, and Josie Morgan, whose family owned the ice-cream van that always parked at Westward Beach. The friends had got to know them both during previous investigations. The two girls were talking excitedly and pointing out to sea.

Emily looked at her watch. They'd been at North Point almost an hour. Vicky and Josie must be the next whale-watch shift. She jumped up, dropping her notebook. They'd got so wrapped up in the case that they'd completely forgotten about the whales! She glanced down at the survey sheet on the clipboard. The last entry was almost fifteen minutes ago! Jack grabbed the camera and Scott picked up the binoculars. Feeling very guilty, all three of them gazed out across the water.

They expected to see the same old seascape: waves, seagulls, fishing boats, a tangle of seaweed floating by ...

What they *didn't* expect to see was a pair of killer whales leaping out of the water, their black backs glistening in the sunshine – as sleek as the paint on the Black Salamander. With a loud slap they plunged back under the water, only to surface again and again in a series of graceful arcs.

'Wow!' Jack breathed. 'It's like something out of a Sea World show!'

'Even better!' Josie panted, as she and Vicky joined Scott, Emily and Jack. 'This is completely natural orca behaviour. How long have they been breaching like this?'

'We, er, only spotted them a couple of seconds before you showed up,' Jack said. *Well, that part's true,* he thought. *Although, for all we know, the whales could*

44

have been doing the conga up and down the channel for the last fourteen and a half minutes!

Vicky smiled. 'It's pretty exciting, isn't it?'

Jack suddenly remembered he was holding the camera and started snapping pictures. The whales were now bobbing up and down with just their heads above the surface as if treading water.

'It's called spy-hopping when they do that,' Josie explained.

Jack and Scott laughed. 'Well, that's made Emily's day!' Scott said. 'Spies in Castle Key!'

As if joining in the joke, the orcas spouted air from their blowholes, clouds of tiny water droplets sparkling in the sunlight. Then they flipped in the air, dived and were gone.

'Phew!' Jack sighed. A new investigation *and* a pair of killer whales. It had been a busy morning and it was still only seven thirty!

—

After a quick detour to fetch Scott's laptop from Stone Cottage, the friends settled down in Emily's small round room on the eighth floor of The Lighthouse to continue working on the case. They quickly agreed that Will Stone, the Black Salamander's back-up driver, was straight in at number one on their list of Suspects We'd Most Like to Interview.

'It's a no-brainer,' Jack said. 'What are we waiting for?'

Scott frowned at his computer screen. He'd found several images of Will Stone on the internet and Emily had confirmed that this was, indeed, the man she'd seen at the Wheel Power test track. He'd also discovered that Stone had been employed as a test driver by Silverwood Cars for the last year, and that he lived near their headquarters in Birmingham. 'We've got to find him first,' he pointed out.

'Birmingham is miles away,' Emily murmured as she made notes. 'Stone must be staying in a hotel or guesthouse somewhere near Carrickstowe while the Black Salamander's at Wheel Power.'

Scott got up from the beanbag and paced round the room. He gazed out of one of the porthole windows across the harbour and the village far below. He yawned and rested his forehead against the cool glass. The crack-of-dawn start was catching up with him. 'There are thousands of hotels in West Cornwall,' he groaned. 'Where do we start?'

Emily was already packing her investigation kit into her bag. 'We'll just have to go back to Wheel Power. With any luck Stone will be there. If not, we'll snoop around and find out where he's staying.'

'And then what?' Scott grumbled. 'We can't just turn up and say "Hey, Will, you don't know us, but have you nicked any amphibious supercars lately?"'

Jack looked up from playing tug-of-war with Drift using a balled-up sock they'd found under Emily's bed. He threw the sock at Scott. 'Thank you, Mr Negative McNegative of Negative City!'

Emily snapped her notebook shut. 'We'll cross that bridge when we come to it!'

Scott couldn't see how they were going to get in through the gates let alone cross any bridges! Security had been tight enough yesterday – it was going to be like a prison camp now a car had gone missing! But he decided to keep his doubts to himself. If Jack said the word *negative* one more time Scott might just throw something at him! And it wouldn't be a sock!

＿

To Scott's surprise the massive Wheel Power gates stood wide open. The friends had parked their bikes a little way down the road, and were now peeping out from a hedge that surrounded a small industrial estate that neighboured the test track.

Two police cars, a South-West TV van and a jeep with *The Carrickstowe Times* logo on its side were queuing up to enter the Wheel Power compound.

'They must have arranged a press conference.' Emily clenched her fists in frustration. 'If only we could get in, we could find out everything the police know about the case!'

Scott shook his head. 'We're not getting in! Not without ID.' He'd been right about the security. A guard was checking each vehicle as it approached the gate before waving it through to the parking area. The queue was building up, stretching back past their observation point. Scott could see in through the window of the South-West TV van crawling to a halt on the road next to them. The driver was leaning on the steering wheel and unwrapping a stick of chewing gum.

Scott turned back to the others, wondering what to do next. Emily was peering through her binoculars at the security guard on the gate. Jack was ...

Scott did a double take.

Jack had disappeared!

Six

Jack Goes it Alone

In fact, Jack was only a few metres away.

Just moments earlier he'd glanced across at the South-West TV van, noticed the back doors weren't shut properly, seen his chance and dived inside, pulling the doors shut behind him – all in the blink of an eye. There'd been no time to bring Scott and Emily in on the move – and no doubt Mr Negative would have come up with all kinds of pointless objections anyway! Now Jack lay wedged uncomfortably among the camera boxes as the van juddered forwards, making its way through the security check and into the compound.

At last he felt the van reverse and park.

Jack torpedoed out of the back and took cover behind a parked car before the van driver had even pulled the handbrake on. He'd hardly got his bearings when he had to leap back to avoid being mown down by a Wheel Power delivery van screeching into the space behind him. He watched as Frank the Forklift climbed out, yawning and stretching and swigging from a takeaway coffee, before heading towards the red brick building along with a steady stream of police officers, reporters and cameramen.

That's when Jack realized he hadn't quite thought this plan through. How was he going to get past the reception desk?

He heard a car door slam and spun round to see Connor Jamison emerge from an awesome red Porsche and stride towards the building. Jack ran after him. It was a long shot but it was the only shot he had! He just hoped Connor wouldn't take him for some kind of crazed stalker-fan and call for security to chuck him out ...

Connor Jamison turned to see who was following him. He frowned for a moment. 'You're one of the kids who was at the track yesterday? Jack, isn't it?'

'Yeah, that's right,' Jack said, trying to sound casual

and totally *not* like a crazed stalker-fan as he fell into step with Connor and entered the building. 'That's tough luck about the Salamander. You must be gutted.'

Connor gave a grim smile. 'You could say that! My chance of being a movie star's gone down the plughole.' He looked stressed out and exhausted, rubbing his hands over his square-jawed face as if trying to scrub away his problems.

The lady at the reception desk glanced at Connor's security pass and waved him through. Jack was about to sidle after him through the door marked *Press Conference* when the receptionist held up a finger.

Jack gulped and stared at the purple-nail-varnished talon. 'I'm here on work experience,' he improvised. *It's not technically a fib*, he thought. *Investigating is hard work and this is definitely an experience!*

The receptionist gave Jack a long, hard look. Then she glanced at the queue of people backing up behind him. At last, with a sigh, she handed him a visitor pass.

Jack darted through the door and found himself in a large meeting room with chairs set out in rows. He slipped into a seat at the back and craned his neck to see over the packed audience. Several people sat at a long table behind a jungle of microphones. Jack recognized Detective Inspector Hassan from Carrickstowe Police. Monty Howard was up there too, along with Connor Jamison, who was just sitting down next to Alesha Rahal. The others at the table were all executive types

51

in suits – no doubt the bigwigs in charge at Silverwood Cars and Wheel Power.

Alesha – who was wearing a bright yellow dress today – stood up and thanked everyone for coming. Jack couldn't help being impressed by her poise. Surely the Black Salamander getting stolen had to be the worst publicity nightmare *ever*, and yet she was smiling at everyone as if welcoming them all to her birthday party.

'Silverwood Cars are offering a *substantial* reward for information leading to the safe return of the Black Salamander,' she said cheerfully before introducing D. I. Hassan, sitting down again and sipping from a coffee mug bearing the motto *Keep Calm and Eat Chocolate*.

D. I. Hassan cleared his throat, smoothed down his thick black moustache and began to brief the reporters about the case. 'This was a sophisticated operation,' he explained. 'The security systems were deactivated so that the alarms didn't go off during the theft. The Black Salamander was found to be missing only when Elizabeth Price, one of the mechanics, arrived to start work on a rush job at four o'clock this morning. We know from the CCTV footage that the Salamander was loaded onto a lorry and driven away shortly after midnight.' D. I. Hassan clicked on a remote control and a grainy video of a white lorry began to play on a screen behind his head. The time stamp on the bottom right-hand corner said 00.15. 'As you can see, it's an ordinary, plain white sixteen-tonner. The number plates are false, of course ...'

The reporters all started firing questions. Suddenly a question of his own started prickling away at the back of Jack's mind – like an itch between his shoulder blades that he just couldn't reach. It was something the security guard had said at the track yesterday ... he needed a coffee because ... yes, that was it ... *he was going to be on the night shift at the track!* Jack's hand began to shoot into the air, but he stopped it just in time. If D. I. Hassan noticed him, he'd be thrown out – or even arrested. Jack didn't know whether sneaking into a press conference was a criminal offence but he was pretty sure it wasn't going to win him any medals.

Jack willed one of the reporters to ask the six-million-dollar question for him, but nobody was picking up his thought-waves. He glanced around, trying frantically to think of something. Suddenly he saw the answer – not the answer to his question but the answer to the question of how to get his question asked! The man in black at the far end of the row was Shane Hazard, the reporter from *Motor Mania*. OK, so they'd only met once, and Shane was technically on the suspect list, but he seemed like a nice guy ...

Jack found a pencil stub and an old Kit Kat wrapper in his shorts pocket and scribbled his question on the back: *Why didn't the security guard do anything?* Then he slid off his seat and began crawling along the row, ignoring the grumbles and the kicks as he squeezed past legs and knocked over bags.

'Psst!' he hissed when he finally reached Shane Hazard's chair. Understandably, the reporter looked a little surprised to find Jack crouching at his feet like a large, friendly dog. He started to say something but Jack cut him off with a frantic lip-zipping gesture. Then he passed up the wrapper.

Shane read the note, nodded, then raised his hand.

D. I. Hassan pointed at him. 'Next question!'

'I assume there was a security guard on duty last night?' Shane said. 'The Black Salamander was stolen just after midnight yet nobody knew about it until four in the morning. Why didn't the guard raise the alarm?'

Couldn't have put it better myself, Jack thought, giving Shane a thumbs-up from under the chair.

D. I. Hassan held up his hands to quell the murmur of excitement that rippled round the room. 'We believe the guard was drugged with a strong sedative. He was only just coming round when the mechanic arrived for work.'

Jack resisted the urge to crowd-surf back to his seat. He couldn't wait to report back to Emily and Scott with all the juicy intel he'd gathered! He'd just started to worm his way back along the row when there was a sudden commotion. Jack froze, his heart banging in his ears. Had D. I. Hassan spotted him?

A chair scraped back and clattered to the floor as a

man in the front row jumped to his feet and bolted for the door.

A man with patchy ginger hair and a scarred face.

His clothes were crumpled and his eyes were red-rimmed and bloodshot.

He looked as if he'd been up all night.

And now he was doing a runner!

Seven

Prime Suspect

They'd looked everywhere.

Emily and Scott had no choice but to admit that Jack was officially missing. Even Drift hadn't been able to sniff him out.

Scott held his head in his hands. Had Jack stumbled through a hidden wormhole into another space-time dimension? Or was he using active camouflage, like the Black Salamander, to blend into the background?

Scott suddenly pictured Jack in next year's *Britain's Got Talent* final: *Jack Carter – The Amazing Chameleon Boy!*

Scott heard Emily say something and snapped back to reality. Knowing Jack, he'd probably charged off on some crazy half-baked mission. And, knowing Jack, it was going to mean trouble.

'Let's go round to the back of the compound,' Emily suggested. 'Max said there was a private harbour. Maybe Jack decided to go and check it out?'

As they walked around the perimeter, Scott kept looking in through the wire fence hoping to catch sight of Jack. But when he finally glimpsed someone dashing across the car park, it wasn't his annoying little brother, but a tall red-haired man in a hurry. He jumped into a classy black convertible and revved the engine.

'Was that—' Emily gasped.

'Will Stone!' Scott cut in.

'Quick! Let's grab our bikes and follow him!'

Scott laughed. 'Hello! Earth calling Emily! He's in a Ferrari Spider. Top speed, one hundred and ninety-three miles per hour. We're on bikes. Top speed, twenty miles an hour with a following wind!'

'But I know where he might be going,' Emily said, already running back towards the front of the compound. Drift raced along at her side, delighted that they were on the move at last!

'How?' Scott laughed. 'Have you got psychic powers all of a sudden?'

'He's staying at the Grand Vista Hotel in Tregower,' Emily called over her shoulder. 'I noticed the sticker for the hotel car park on the windscreen of that Ferrari when we were here yesterday. I just didn't know it belonged to Will Stone!'

Scott jogged after her. 'But what's to say he's even going back to the hotel?'

'It's worth a try!' Emily shouted. 'If he crosses the causeway onto Castle Key island we can be pretty sure that's where he's headed.' She flew round the corner and barrelled straight into Jack who was sprinting out of the main gates. Drift yipped in surprise and Scott skidded to a halt just in time to avoid ploughing into them.

'Will Stone's on the run!' Jack yelled as he picked himself up.

'Will Stone's on the run!' Scott and Emily shouted at the same time.

The three friends looked at each other and laughed. 'I know!' they all said in chorus. Without another word they ran to their bikes and unlocked them. Clumsy with haste, their fingers fumbled to twist the combination locks, but at last the numbers clicked into place. Drift hopped up into his basket. Together they bombed down the road. But when they reached the causeway there was no sign of the Ferrari.

'Too late!' Jack groaned. 'We've lost him!'

'Who's being Mr Negative now?' Scott asked. 'Listen!'

Jack put his hand behind his ear. Then he nodded and grinned. 'The unmistakable growl of the V8 engine,' he said dramatically, impersonating a *Top Gear* presenter. 'Yes, it's the Ferrari Spider!'

'And it's coming from the Castle Key end of the causeway!' Emily shouted as she pedalled off so fast that Drift almost shot out of the basket.

—

Scott, Jack and Emily raced to Tregower, a village on the north-west coast of the island. They screeched along the seafront, propped their bikes against the war memorial, hurried across the road and hurtled up the front steps of the super-elegant Grand Vista Hotel.

A brand new revolving glass door had been installed. Still gasping for breath, Emily peered through the glass.

'Yes!' she murmured.

Will Stone was standing in the lobby talking on his mobile. Nearby, a young man in a green waistcoat with gold buttons was scowling at a computer screen behind the check-in counter. Emily's heart sank. It was Omar! Last time they were here, she and Jack had spun Omar a not-entirely-true tale about being the niece and nephew of a missing rock star. They'd also climbed out through a second floor window. Emily had a feeling

Omar wasn't going to welcome them back with open arms.

'You'll have to go in,' she urged Scott. 'You're the only one Omar won't recognize.' Before Scott could object, he found himself propelled into the revolving door by a firm shove in the back. He tried continuing all the way round to the outside again but Jack and Emily blocked his escape.

'Go on!' Jack hissed, giving the door a hefty push. 'Don't be a wimp!'

Scott catapulted into the lobby like a ball shooting into a pinball machine.

It was like walking – or rather staggering – onto the set of a historical drama: all wood panelling, glitzy chandeliers and tinkling piano music. Ladies looked up from their afternoon tea and muttered softly about young people and bad manners.

Still a little dizzy, Scott shuffled towards a noticeboard and pretended to study a poster about the Tregower flower festival. Out of the corner of his eye, he watched Will Stone, who was pacing up and down talking into his phone.

'I'll be there as soon as I can!' he was saying. 'I can't wait to celebrate our special delivery!'

Oh, yeah, this is it! Scott thought. The 'special delivery' had to be the Black Salamander! Suddenly Scott realized he was staring at Will Stone. He quickly looked away but it was too late. Stone had glanced across the lobby and was now looking straight at him. Scott's stomach lurched. If Stone rumbled that Scott was earwigging on him talking to his criminal contacts, he wasn't going to let him walk free to tell the police all about it, that was for sure!

But to Scott's relief Will Stone turned back towards the check-in desk.

Scott focused on the flower festival poster and tried to get his galloping heartbeat back under control.

'You'd like to check out? Certainly, sir!' Omar took Stone's credit card and tapped at his keyboard. 'I'll send someone up to get your bags.'

'No need. I'll run up and get them myself,' Stone said. He dashed away up the staircase taking the stairs two at a time.

'Can I help you?'

Scott spun round to see Omar looking at him with raised eyebrows. He mumbled the first thing that came into his head. 'I've got a message for Will Stone.'

Omar held out his hand. 'You just missed him. Leave it with me.'

'Er, my instructions were to deliver it in person ...'

Omar made a suit-yourself face. 'OK. Mr Stone should be down again soon.'

Scott sank down on a creaky leather sofa and tried desperately to cook up a message that sounded remotely plausible. If Stone realized that Scott was on to him and his 'special delivery' the game would be up. He was seriously considering making a run for the door when Will Stone came bounding back into the lobby carrying a holdall. He spoke to Omar then hurried over to Scott.

'You have a message for me?' he asked, then smiled. 'Oh, I thought I recognized you just now. You were at the track yesterday, weren't you? Sorry, but I'm in a bit of a rush. My wife's just had a baby.'

'A *baby*?' Scott parroted.

Will Stone grinned and flopped down on the sofa next to Scott. 'Yeah, you know? Small wriggly things. They wear nappies. Cry a lot!' He yawned. 'I think I'd better stop for a strong coffee on the way home. I drove back to Birmingham last night and got there just in time to see the baby being born. Then I got a call at five o'clock this morning to say the Salamander had disappeared so I had to turn around and drive back here to Cornwall. But I can't stay any longer – my wife needs me there.'

Scott stared at Will Stone as the truth slowly dawned on him. The *special delivery* was a baby! 'So ... you weren't here when the Black Salamander was stolen?' he stammered.

Will shrugged. 'Nope! Like I told the police, I was in Birmingham Maternity Hospital from eleven last night.'

'So who do you think did it?' Scott couldn't help asking.

Will shook his head sadly. 'I don't know. I just hope they're treating her right. She's a very special machine.

One thing I do know. It has to be an inside job. Someone must have deactivated the security alarms and—' He broke off, looked at his watch and jumped up from the sofa again. 'So, what was the message you had for me?' he asked.

Scott stood up. 'Oh, it was just to say congratulations on the new baby,' he improvised. 'From, er, Connor Jamison,' he added, saying the first name he could think of.

A shadow flickered across Will Stone's face, but then he gave a lopsided smile. 'Cheers! That's cool. Connor and I used to be good mates but I've been really down on him ever since he got picked to be the driver for the movie instead of me. Still, I guess it's not Connor's fault that Alesha thought he'd be a better image for Silverwood Cars than old Frankenstein's Monster here.'

Scott nodded sympathetically, remembering Alesha's words to Emily: *a pretty face will broaden market appeal*. Will was definitely not a pretty face but he seemed like a good guy. 'Could I have your autograph, please?' he asked on impulse.

Will Stone smiled. He pulled a business card from his wallet, scrawled on the back and handed it to Scott. Then he grabbed his holdall and disappeared through the door.

Scott felt a tap on the shoulder and turned to see Omar. He jumped, expecting to be thrown out for making the hotel look untidy.

'I saw you looking at the flower festival poster,' Omar said. 'Thought you might like one of these.' He thrust a leaflet into Scott's hand.

Scott took it, mumbled his thanks and hurried out of the hotel.

'What happened?' Emily demanded, ambushing Scott as soon as he emerged onto the steps.

Scott was about to answer when Jack jumped in. 'What have you got there?' He snatched the leaflet from Scott's hand. 'An entry form for a flower arranging competition!' He snorted with disbelief. 'Call yourself an investigator? Our prime suspect has escaped and you're more interested in *flowers*?'

Scott grabbed the leaflet back, crumpled it into a ball and fired it into a litter bin.

Eight

Teamwork

Jack staggered away from the hotel towards his bike. 'Lu-u-u-u-nch!' he moaned. 'My stomach's forgotten what food looks like!'

Scott was famished too. It was almost two o'clock and they'd been up since five. 'Let's go to Westward Beach and I'll update you there,' he suggested. 'That little kiosk on the seafront has great Cornish pasties.'

'And Drift can have a run on the beach while we

debrief and analyze the morning's progress,' Emily added.

In the bike basket, Drift flicked up one ear – the white one with brown spots. He didn't understand everything Emily said, of course (but then, nor did Scott or Jack), but he recognized the words *run* and *beach*. What more did a dog need?

Equipped with pasties, Cokes and cream cakes the friends trotted down the wooden steps onto the long stretch of pale golden sand. While Drift raced up and down barking at crabs, they flopped down and wolfed their picnic. At the other end of the beach a crowd of small children had gathered around a Punch and Judy show. Distant shrieks of laughter mingled with the crying of the gulls and the rolling of the waves.

'Ahhh! That's better!' Jack sighed, tipping the last crumbs into his mouth. 'Now, who wants to hear all about my daring solo mission into enemy territory?'

'You mean getting into the press conference?' Emily laughed. She took out her notebook and wrote like crazy as Jack recounted his story – ending with the CCTV footage of the lorry with the exact time of the theft and the fact that the security guard had been drugged.

'And that's when Will Stone jumped up and ran out! Suspicious or what?' Jack finished.

'I knew it!' Emily cried. 'When I heard him on the phone at the track he was planning it all with his accomplices ... *tonight's the night.*'

'Sorry to spoil your lovely theory,' Scott said, draining the last of his Coke, 'but Stone's no longer a suspect. He was talking to his wife.' Jack and Emily listened in astonishment as Scott explained that Will Stone had a rock-solid alibi for the time the Salamander was stolen – an entire maternity hospital full of doctors and nurses could vouch for him. 'He rushed out of the press conference to get back to Birmingham to his wife and new baby.'

Emily shook her head glumly. Babies were fine, she supposed, but she'd much rather have a decent prime suspect! As she took her ruler and crossed Will Stone off the suspect list she couldn't help feeling a bit left out. She was the only one with no new intelligence to report. For a moment she missed the old days when she and Drift had worked alone. But only for a moment. She couldn't imagine running an investigation without the boys now. *It's all about teamwork*, she reminded herself. And there was plenty of work to be done! 'Let's each follow one of the other suspects on the list to see if they're up to anything,' she said. 'There's Alesha Rahal for a start ...'

Jack laughed. 'Ooh, I bet Scott will volunteer to follow Alesha. He really fancies her!'

'Do *not*!' Scott protested.

Jack picked up a stick and drew a heart in the sand. Then he scrawled SC 4 AR across the middle. 'We all saw you go red when she said you looked like something out of a boy band!'

Scott leaped up and scrubbed out the heart with his foot. 'I'm not the slightest bit interested in Alesha!'

'In that case you won't mind following someone else!' Jack scanned Emily's list for the most boring-looking option. 'Like old Frank the fork-lift driver!'

Scott shrugged to show he didn't care.

Jack grinned and looked back down the list for the most interesting suspect for himself. 'Aha! I'll shadow Shane Hazard.' He figured a reporter for a car magazine was bound to have a dead exciting day: driving cool cars, doing interviews with racing drivers, chatting to TV presenters ... 'And that leaves Alesha for Emily.'

'Just watch out for the Killer Hairbrush!' Scott joked.

Emily batted him with her notebook. 'Now, how are we going to get back into Wheel Power to tail these suspects? Any ideas?'

There was no reply. Emily looked up from her notes. Scott had stretched out on the sand and was snoring softly. Curled up at his side, Drift snuffled in his sleep. Herding crabs was hard work! And as for Jack, he'd disappeared – again! But this time his whereabouts were no mystery. He was halfway to the ice-cream van!

'Part-timer!' Emily called after him.

Jack turned and walked backwards. 'I'm going to get an update on the killer whale situation from Josie!' he shouted. 'She's working in the van today.'

'Not trying to wangle a free ice cream then,' Emily laughed.

'Wouldn't dream of it!'

Emily sighed. So much for teamwork! She closed her eyes – just for a moment – while she tried to think of a plan.

When she woke up, Scott and Jack and Drift were playing piggy-in-the-middle with an old tennis ball they'd found, their shadows sliding across the sand, as long as if they were on stilts. It was too late for any more investigating today. Even Punch and Judy had packed up and gone home.

Emily sprang up, raced round in front of Jack and caught the ball out of his hands.

—

By next morning the friends had finally come up with a plan and now they were putting it into action.

So far, it was working perfectly. Emily had phoned the Wheel Power test track and asked for Alesha Rahal. She'd told Alesha that she and the boys thought they'd seen something when they were visiting the test track that might be relevant to the case of the stolen Black Salamander. They didn't want to go to the police, Emily said, in case they were wrong and got an innocent person into trouble.

Just as they'd hoped, Alesha had suggested that they come and tell her all about it – which is how Scott, Jack and Emily came to be sitting in Alesha's office with visitor passes hanging round their necks. They'd decided to leave Drift at The Lighthouse again so that he wouldn't be frightened by the engine noise at the test track.

The small room in the red brick building was only a temporary base for Alesha while she was stationed at Wheel Power. One end was filled with metal filing cabinets and shelves of folders, but she'd customized the area around her desk with a long mirror and a collection of little plaques inscribed with helpful sayings like PROBLEMS ARE NOT STOP SIGNS, THEY ARE GUIDELINES and THE DARKER THE SKY, THE BRIGHTER THE RAINBOW.

'So what did you want to tell me?' Alesha asked, looking up from a wafer-thin pink laptop.

Emily smiled. This was the part of the plan they were most proud of. Their 'information' had to be something believably important but totally useless at the same time. Alesha was still a suspect, after all. If she'd been involved in stealing the Salamander they couldn't risk telling her anything that would help her get away with it. And – this was the most brilliant part of all – it wasn't even a lie!

'Well, it was when we were here with Max,' Emily began in a worried voice. 'I spotted this strange-looking man – later, we figured out it was Will Stone – talking to someone on the phone and acting very suspiciously. I couldn't help overhearing him saying that he was fed up with Connor getting to drive the Salamander for the movie ... He sounded really angry about not being picked.'

'So, when we heard about the Salamander being stolen, we wondered whether Stone could have something to do with it,' Scott chipped in.

'You know, to get his *revenge*!' Jack added with a theatrical touch.

Alesha smiled. 'I like your thinking, guys. Two ambitious young Formula One drivers, they're best buddies, one horribly scarred in an accident, the other goes on to fame and fortune – it's got primetime mini-series written all over it.' She paused and shook her head. 'But I'm afraid Stone didn't steal the Salamander.'

'How do you know?' Scott asked innocently.

'He was with his wife last night having a baby. It's a nice little human interest story, of course, but it's not a Revenge Tragedy.'

Emily tried to look surprised. 'Oh, that's a relief! I'm so glad we didn't go to the police and make fools of ourselves!'

Alesha smiled. 'No harm done!' She glanced at her gold Gucci watch. 'I've got a crew coming in from an American news network to do a to-camera piece. The Salamander's disappearance has gone global.' She stood up and looked in the mirror, smoothing down the fitted white dress and jacket that set off her dark hair and golden-brown skin. She held a scarf up to her throat.

'What do you think? It's coral but will it come up *peach* on film? Peach is a no-no! Or how about this?' She took a red scarf from her desk and draped it round her neck. 'Too shouty?'

'Do you have to wear a scarf at all?' Emily asked. She couldn't seen the point of scarves – apart from woolly ones to keep you warm in winter. Surely those floaty ones just wafted around and got in the way.

Alesha whipped the red scarf off and studied her reflection. 'You are *so* right! Less is more!'

So far, so good, Emily thought. Now, for the next – and possibly most difficult – phase of the plan: to keep Alesha talking while the boys escaped to spy on Shane Hazard and the forklift driver. 'I've always wanted to work in public relations,' she said. 'Could I ask you a few questions about how you got started?'

'Sure,' Alesha said, as she twisted the top off a red lipstick. 'I have a few moments while I get ready. It's nice to have some female company for a change. There's Lizzy Price, of course, but she's more into engine oil than girl talk.'

Emily shot a look at Scott and Jack. This was their cue!

'We'll just go and, er, look at the cars, shall we?' Scott said. 'Leave you to your *girl talk*!' He tugged Jack's sleeve and they headed for the door.

Emily studied a mug on the desk as if fascinated by the motto printed on the side: WHEN LIFE GIVES

YOU LEMONS, MAKE LEMONADE. She knew the boys were sniggering their heads off; Emily wasn't exactly a *girl talk* kind of girl! Well, she'd show them! A good undercover agent could deal with any challenge.

'I like your earrings!' she began, in her best girl talk manner.

'First rule of public relations,' Alesha explained. 'Always look your best!'

'Ooh, I'll write that down,' Emily said, taking out her notebook.

'In fact, we could do something with your hair ...'

Scott and Jack backed out of the office before Emily could change her mind!

Nine

Surveillance Operations

The boys headed for the track and stood at the barrier watching the cars rocket round. Suddenly Scott felt an elbow in his ribs.

'There goes your man!' Jack hissed, as Frank the forklift driver hurried towards the Portakabin on the other side of the compound and disappeared inside.

'I'm on it!' Scott said, following the stout figure

in blue overalls. When he came to the Portakabin, he stood on the steps up to the door and peeped in through the glass panel. Inside was a small lounge that looked like a school staff room, except that the coffee table was piled with motoring magazines instead of reports and there were posters of racing cars on the walls rather than notices about headlice and nut allergies. Frank was feeding coins into a vending machine in the corner. He grabbed his coffee and a Mars bar and headed straight back out – almost bumping into Scott on the steps.

'Just going to, er, get a drink,' Scott mumbled, fishing a pound coin out of his pocket and holding it up as evidence.

Moments later Scott came back out of the Portakabin with a can of Cherry Coke. He didn't even like Cherry Coke but it was the only cold drink left in the machine. He saw Frank stop to talk to Connor Jamison for a moment, before sitting down on a bench outside one of the large storage sheds to eat his snack and read *The Carrickstowe Times*. Scott had to creep the long way round the back of the buildings to get near without being seen. He found a good vantage point between two lorries. Eventually, Frank stood up, brushed crumbs from his double chin and entered the storage shed through a metal roll-down door.

Still clutching the Cherry Coke, Scott sneaked in after him. He ducked behind a crate marked *Steel Crash Barriers* and watched as Frank hauled himself up into a bright yellow forklift truck. With a chorus of warning beeps, he reversed down a wide aisle between shelves of car supplies, scooped up an oil drum on the fork attachment, transported it to the other side of the warehouse and lowered it to the floor.

Then he went back and shifted another oil drum.

Scott groaned. This had to be the most boring stake-out ever! And it was all Jack's fault! If Jack hadn't started going on about him fancying Alesha he could be watching her do her interview instead of crouching behind a dusty crate watching a truck moving stuff around. And no doubt Jack was having a blast tailing Shane Hazard. He was probably having lunch with Jeremy Clarkson or test-driving the latest model Aston Martin by now ...

—

In fact, Jack was even more bored than Scott! It had all looked so promising. He'd spotted Shane Hazard talking to Elizabeth Price, the mechanic, outside one of the workshops, so he'd scooted over and hidden behind a pile of old tyres, confident he was about to overhear some juicy details that would crack the case wide open. Were they working out how to move the Black Salamander to a new secret location? Or even plotting to steal another car?

No such luck! Shane Hazard and Elizabeth Price

turned out to be discussing new government guidelines on fuel prices.

And they kept it up for fifteen whole soul-destroying minutes!

At last, Shane Hazard said goodbye and headed for the lounge in the Portakabin. Jack leaned against the wall outside, pretending to have a long conversation on his mobile phone, every now and then glancing in through the window. Shane pushed his sunglasses up onto his head, bought a coffee from the machine, sat down and began typing on his laptop. This was so dull it made flower-arranging sound like a thrill-fest! What about test-driving supercars? What about lunching with celebrities? Jack vowed he'd never buy another copy of *Motor Mania* magazine in protest.

Jack was about to give up when Shane Hazard's phone rang. *At last!* This could be the boss of the car-stealing crime ring telling Shane where to take the Salamander. Or, at least, Jeremy Clarkson inviting him to lunch!

Shane Hazard's eyes darted around as if checking nobody could hear him. Jack ducked his head below the windowsill just in time. When he peeped in again Shane had turned his back to the window. Jack pressed his ear to the glass.

'You've got something for me?' Shane asked in a low voice. 'OK. Five minutes.' He closed his laptop, flipped down his sunglasses and started for the door.

Jack's pulse revved like a turbo-charged V8 engine. This was more like it!

—

Meanwhile, Alesha had brushed and braided Emily's hair beyond recognition. Emily smiled through gritted teeth. *All in the line of duty*, she told herself. She stared at the mug on the desk: WHEN LIFE GIVES YOU LEMONS, MAKE LEMONADE.

'That's my personal motto!' Alesha said. 'It means you have to make the best of things – you know, turn sour into sweet.'

What do you think I'm doing right now? Emily thought grimly as the hairbrush snagged on yet another tangle. *This is perfect training for resisting torture by enemy agents if I'm ever captured and interrogated.*

When Alesha was finally satisfied with Emily's hairstyle and her own make-up, she stuffed her laptop in her bag and hurried out to meet the American news crew near the track. Emily tagged along.

Halfway across the compound Alesha suddenly stopped. 'Darn it! I've forgotten the information packs I wanted to hand out.'

'I'll run back and get them for you,' Emily offered.

'Would you? What an angel!'

Beneath her best angelic smile Emily wasn't in danger of earning a halo any time soon. She was thinking a decidedly *un-angelic* thought: *Perfect! A chance to snoop around Alesha's office!*

She sprinted back and let herself in using the six-digit code that Alesha had whispered to her. She took her stopwatch from her bag and set it for five minutes. Any longer and she risked Alesha coming to look for her.

Emily began riffling through the folders and filing cabinets.

But, to her disappointment, Emily soon realized that none of the files belonged to Alesha Rahal. *Of course!* she fumed. This wasn't Alesha's usual office. She would keep all her paperwork back at Silverwood HQ in Birmingham. These were just routine copies of delivery notes and orders for supplies going in and out of Wheel Power.

She glanced at her stopwatch. She had three minutes left.

She was closing the drawer of the filing cabinet when she noticed a page that was sticking up a little. Without thinking, she pulled it out and gave it a quick glance.

Box containing customized carbon-fibre hubcaps
Delivered from Wheel Power to Auto-Dynamic
Manufacturing, Weymouth
Driver: Frank Evans
Date: August 20th

Emily wasn't sure what a carbon-fibre hubcap was,

but she did know important evidence when she saw it.

The note was stamped with the words *Overnight Delivery* and August twentieth was the night the Black Salamander had disappeared.

Frank Evans? That had to be Frank the forklift driver. And if he'd been delivering hubcaps to Weymouth that night then he couldn't have been stealing the Salamander at the same time. He had a perfect alibi! *Or did he?* Emily wondered. Wasn't it just a little too convenient that he was out on an overnight delivery the very night of the crime? Could it be a cover story? What if Frank had really been driving the lorry with the GPS tracker on board to Plymouth, while his accomplice drove the Salamander to a secret location?

She had two minutes left.

—

This is a total waste of time, Scott thought, as the forklift ferried yet another oil drum across the warehouse. The concrete floor was rock hard and his right foot had the worst case of pins and needles in living memory. *I've had enough of this!* He waited until the forklift was heading away towards the shelves then slid out from behind the crate and began creeping towards the exit.

Hearing the whine of an engine behind him, Scott spun round. The forklift was speeding towards him, its two long, flat pointed tines raised to chest height like a pair of giant bayonets. Gripped by terror, he stared at the blades. He was going to be impaled!

Scott could smell the metal, almost feel its cold touch. Just in time, he dived back behind the crate. He poked his head out. The truck was still coming straight at him! *But surely Frank must have seen me!* Scott thought. The warehouse was brightly lit by strip lights hanging from the ceiling. *Is he blind or something?* At least now he wouldn't be skewered by the fork like a human kebab. The crate would take the impact; it was full of crash barriers, after all! But Scott's relief lasted no longer than a single heartbeat. He hadn't escaped – he'd walked into a trap!

The forklift was pushing the crate against the wall.

The crate was closing in on him.

He was going to be crushed until all that was left of him was a sticky splat on the wall, like a freshly swatted fly. Already he could feel splinters of rough wood prickling his skin.

Scott screamed at the top of his lungs, 'Help!'

Ten

Partners in Crime

Meanwhile, Emily was still in Alesha's office staring at the delivery note. It was for the night the Black Salamander had disappeared and it had Frank Evans' name on it. Was she looking at a watertight alibi or a brilliant cover story?

There was only one way to find out.

The number for Auto-Dynamic in Weymouth was on the delivery note. Emily grabbed the phone from

Alesha's desk and punched in the number. 'Come on!' she muttered through her teeth. 'Pick up the phone!' She only had fifty seconds left before her stopwatch would beep to tell her to get out.

At last a man answered.

'I'm calling from Wheel Power,' Emily said in an official-sounding voice. 'We're just following up on some of our recent deliveries. Did you receive your hubcaps on time on the twentieth of August?'

There was the sound of a teaspoon stirring something in a mug at the other end of the line. 'Oh, yes,' the man said. 'I took delivery of them myself. Just before five in the morning it was. I'm not usually here that early, mind, but we were waiting for those hubcaps to come back from testing at Wheel Power for a big rush job we'd got on.'

Emily made a vague *uh-huh* sound as if she were ticking boxes on a form. 'And did the driver give his name?'

'He didn't have to give his name, love! It was Frank Evans. Old Frank's back and forth up here all the time with deliveries from Wheel Power. Usually stops for a cuppa before he heads back down to Carrickstowe.'

Emily puffed out her breath. It all checked out. Frank Evans was in the clear! She knew she should say thank you and goodbye – she only had twenty seconds left – but she'd just thought of something. What if Frank drove the lorry to Plymouth with the GPS tracker on board, then handed it over to another driver to take onto the ferry? He could have hired a van at the ferry terminal and continued on to Weymouth to make his delivery. 'Just one last question,' she said. 'What kind of vehicle was Frank driving?'

There was a spluttering sound as if the man's tea or coffee had gone down the wrong way. 'What do you think he was driving? One of your Wheel Power delivery vans, of course! What did you say this was about again, love?' he added, beginning to sound more than a little suspicious.

'It's a customer satisfaction survey,' Emily said, reciting a phrase she'd heard a telemarketing caller use on the phone at home a few days ago. 'You've been most helpful! Bye!'

The stopwatch beeped as she hung up. She'd been in Alesha's office for five minutes. She wiped the phone with a tissue to remove fingerprint evidence, snatched up the forgotten information packs from the desk and flew out of the door.

Emily found Alesha near the test circuit with a small crowd gathered around her, including two cameramen and a sound engineer brandishing a huge microphone covered with a grey fluffy wind-muffler.

Alesha waved Emily over and thanked her. She smiled at the crew. 'This is Emily, my assistant for the day! At Silverwood Cars we think it's *so* important to engage with the younger generation.' She took the information packs and handed them round. 'Now, if you'll excuse me, I need a bathroom break. Back in ten!'

Emily waited a moment and then sneaked after her. Alesha hurried into the red brick building, but instead of turning off towards the toilets she continued down the corridor. She glanced over her shoulder. Emily pressed herself into a corner out of view, her heart in her mouth. Alesha looked around once again before disappearing into a room. Emily tiptoed along the corridor. She would have loved to follow Alesha through the door – which was marked STORES – but from the way Alesha was acting, whatever was happening in that storeroom wasn't exactly a public event.

Suddenly Emily heard footsteps coming along the corridor. Not wanting to be caught lurking with her ear pressed against the storeroom door, she pulled open the next door along and slipped inside. Maybe she'd be able to hear something through the wall.

The door closed behind her.

It was pitch black.

Something brushed against her face.

Emily sprang back against the door, her heart now trying to pound its way out of her chest. *There was someone standing right behind the door!*

She jumped again as her knee touched something soft and layers of material flapped around her.

With shaking hands Emily pulled her torch from her bag and shone it around. She almost laughed out loud.

She was in a cloakroom full of spare overalls hanging from a rail! Behind them, shelves were stacked with racing helmets and high-visibility jackets.

Still trembling a little, Emily took out her brand new micro-listening device. She hooked the plastic earpiece over her ear and unrolled the cable that attached it to a tiny microphone fitted inside a suction pad. She stuck the pad onto the wall that adjoined the storeroom and switched the device on.

—

Meanwhile, Jack was shadowing Shane Hazard. As soon as he'd taken the call, the reporter jogged down the steps of the Portakabin, sauntered across the compound with his hands in his pockets and entered the red brick building by a side door.

Ooh, I bet he's set up an interview with a really famous racing driver, Jack 'The Shadow' Carter thought as he sneaked into the building and ducked behind a water-cooler. He watched Shane walk down a corridor, check his watch and glance around in a highly shifty manner, before going through a door. *Wow!* The Shadow thought. *It must be a mega-celebrity who's here undercover. It could be Michael Schumacher. Or even The Stig!*

The Shadow hovered outside the door. He leaned closer and put his ear to the wood. 'Pants!' he muttered. He couldn't hear a thing. There weren't even any glass panels or keyholes to peep through. So near and yet so far! And now he could hear voices coming along the corridor. One of them sounded like that scary receptionist with the purple talons. Jack didn't even have to think about it; years of experience of dodging patrolling teachers in corridors kicked in. He picked a door at random and ducked inside.

Blinking in the dark, Jack felt along the wall for a light switch. Suddenly his fingers bumped into something. *Uggh! Was that hair? And skin?* He snatched his hand back, his mind working overtime. *Maybe the thieves who stole the Salamander hadn't just drugged a security guard. Maybe they'd killed another one and stashed the body in this cupboard ...* Cautiously he felt again. This time he touched something truly horrible. A warm, slimy eyeball!

'Ouch!'

Hang on, dead bodies don't say ouch!

'Agggghhhmmmmmppppfff!' Jack's scream was cut off by a hand clamping itself over his mouth. He thought his heart would explode with terror.

A voice hissed at him out of the dark. A voice that said, 'Jack, shut *up!*'

'Mmmmpppppffff!' Jack said.

The hand unclamped itself.

'Emily?' Jack whimpered.

Emily illuminated her face with the torch beam. 'You just poked me in the eye!'

'Sorry!' Jack whispered. 'I was only messing about with the screaming and everything,' he added quickly. 'I knew it was you all the time!'

Emily grinned. 'Of course you did.' She pointed at the wall that divided the cloakroom from the storeroom. 'Alesha's meeting someone in there.'

'Shane's meeting someone in there, too!'

The two friends stared at each other, eyes wide, like a pair of startled bush-babies in the torchlight. 'Alesha and Shane,' Jack gasped. 'Secret rendezvous. Partners in crime!'

'Shh!' Emily hissed, handing him the earpiece. 'You listen. I've spotted an air vent up there I might be able to see through with my periscope.' She reached into her bag, took out a black tube that looked like a bike pump and extended it like a telescope.

'And you just happened to have a periscope in your bag?' Jack started to ask. But then he gave up. This was Emily. Of course she did! She probably had an entire submarine in there, let alone a periscope!

Emily grinned as she put her eye to the eyepiece. 'They sell them for looking over the crowds at golf tournaments and things,' she whispered. 'But who'd want to waste one of these on watching *golf*?' She turned the eyepiece to adjust the focus. 'Yes,' she whispered. 'I can see them.'

'What are they doing?' Jack asked, bursting with impatience.

'Kissing!' Emily groaned.

'Yuk!' Jack was disgusted. He'd been trapped in a scene from a zombie film all for the sake of a soppy secret smooch-a-thon!

'They've stopped now,' Emily whispered. 'Can you hear them talking yet?'

Jack joggled the earpiece. There was a swishing and crackling, then Shane's voice.

'You said you had a story for me? Have the police made a breakthrough?'

Jack edged closer to Emily so that she could hear too.

'Not yet,' Alesha sighed. 'They keep telling us they're following enquiries.'

'So what is it? I can't hang around doing interviews about fuel prices for much longer,' Shane complained.

'I think you should follow up the Rick Sullivan angle.'

'But that's old news,' Shane said. 'He wanted to buy the Salamander for his collection a few months ago, but Silverwood wouldn't sell it to him. End of story.'

'OK. Don't say where you heard this,' Alesha replied, 'but Sullivan made another even bigger offer last week, just before he went off to Beijing on business. Silverwood refused again, but ...'

'You think Sullivan might have got tired of hearing no for an answer and decided to help himself?' Shane Hazard asked. 'Do you have any evidence?'

'No,' Alesha admitted. 'But even if there's nothing in it, there's no harm in bandying Rick Sullivan's name about a bit. It always grabs media attention! Look, I have to get back to the news interview now ...'

It went quiet. Jack took off the earpiece. 'Let me guess,' he groaned. 'More kissing?'

Emily looked up from the periscope, her right eye ringed with a red mark from the eyepiece. She made a face and nodded. 'Snorkel-grade snogging.'

Emily eased open the door of the cloakroom and peeped out into the corridor. 'Coast's clear!' she whispered.

'Let's find Scott and get out of here,' Jack said. 'It must be lunchtime.'

Jack and Emily hurried out of the building and across the compound to the trackside. There was no sign of Scott.

'Probably got bored and went home. No staying power,' Jack grumbled as they walked past the doors of a large storage shed.

'Help!'

Jack looked at Emily. 'That sounded like ...'

'Scott!' they cried, running into the warehouse past a stack of oil drums. A forklift truck was pushing a big wooden crate marked *Steel Crash Barriers* up against the wall. It scraped over the concrete floor like fingernails on a blackboard.

'Scott!' Jack yelled. 'You in here?'

'Help!' The voice came from behind the crate.

'Stop!' Jack screamed. He ran towards the forklift. Like a scene from a nightmare monster-chase, his legs seemed to be moving in slow motion, as if he were wading through treacle. 'My brother's trapped back there!' he yelled.

Now Emily was at his side, jumping up and down, waving her arms.

Frank Evans looked down from the cab. He looked baffled for a moment, then his plump face twisted with horror. He pulled a switch and the forklift juddered to a halt. The engine noise stopped.

In the sudden silence the muffled pop of an explosion sounded from behind the crate. Dark red liquid spattered across the metallic grey wall.

It was too late.

Jack fell to his knees, beating his fists against the side of the forklift, hating every millimetre of its stupidly cheerful bright yellow paintwork.

'You've burst Scott!' he sobbed.

Eleven

Scott's Lucky Talisman

'But you don't even *like* Cherry Coke!' Jack laughed. 'I do now,' Scott said, turning the crushed can over in his hand. 'It might just have saved my life.'

The noise behind the crate hadn't been Scott popping like human bubble wrap, after all! It was the can of Cherry Coke from the vending machine. At the last second he'd wedged it between the crate and a ledge that he'd spotted sticking out a little way from the wall next to him. The can had crumpled and exploded, but it had slowed the crate for a fraction of a second – which turned out to be just long enough for Frank Evans to jam the brakes on the forklift. Scott had staggered out – white-faced, quaking and covered in Cherry Coke – but still alive.

Frank Evans had leaped down from the cab and run to Scott's side. 'I'm so sorry, I didn't see you there!' he kept saying. But once it was clear that Scott was unharmed, the driver's shock turned into anger. 'What do you think you were doing wandering around the warehouse? Didn't you see the CAUTION signs? Why weren't you wearing a high-visibility jacket?'

Scott had been incapable of speech. Jack and Emily had mumbled apologies and excuses about Scott getting lost and then bundled him out of the warehouse before Frank could ask any more questions about what they were up to.

They'd cycled straight back to The Lighthouse where Drift had greeted them with a kamikaze bark-and-lick ambush, as if they'd been gone for weeks rather than hours. Jack made sandwiches while Scott went off to wash the Cherry Coke out of his hair and Emily found him a clean t-shirt of her dad's to put on.

They'd brought their sandwiches outside and were now sitting on the rocks at the end of the promontory looking out over Key Bay.

Emily took out her notebook. 'We've got a lot of

new information to sort out ...' Suddenly she stopped. 'Hang on, I've just got to do something.' She stood up, bent over and shook her head so violently that her whole body joined in – just like Drift drying his fur after a swim. Hairgrips pinged in all directions as her chestnut curls burst free of Alesha's handiwork. 'That's better!' she sighed, sitting back down. 'Now, where were we?'

'Frank is obviously the one who stole the Black Salamander,' Scott said. 'He must have clocked I was on to him and was trying to silence me for good! Move him up to the top of the suspect list.'

Emily frowned. 'But Frank Evans has an alibi for the night the Salamander disappeared.' She explained how she'd found the delivery note in Alesha's office and phoned the Auto-Dynamic factory. 'It all checked out. Frank was driving the Wheel Power delivery van taking hubcaps to Weymouth. He can't have been driving the lorry to Plymouth at the same time.'

'You mean I risked my life tailing a suspect you already knew was off the hook?' Scott snapped.

'But I didn't know you were ...' Emily began

'... in a tight spot!' Jack chipped in, roaring with laughter at his own joke.

'... in trouble,' Emily went on. 'Otherwise I'd have texted to tell you he was eliminated from our enquiries.'

'And anyway,' Jack pointed out, 'we were busy as well, following Alesha and Shane.' He grinned. 'I nearly died of fright when I bumped into Emily in the cloakroom!'

Scott threw down his sandwich. 'While you two were playing sardines in the cupboard I was nearly eliminated from the *planet*!'

Emily patted Scott's arm. She'd have given him a hug but decided it would be too soppy. 'I know you've been through a horrible experience, but it was an accident. You saw Frank's face. He was in shock, too. And there's nothing else to link him to the theft.'

'You want to stick to flower arranging, mate,' Jack laughed. 'Much safer!'

Scott scrambled to his feet. He marched to the end of the promontory and stood with his arms folded, glaring out to sea. Drift padded after him and nudged his nose gently against Scott's knee; he hated it when one of the friends was upset. Scott acknowledged Drift with a quick pat but he didn't budge. He could have been killed and Jack and Emily wouldn't care. They were laughing at him. And what was worse, they might be right. Maybe it *was* an accident, not a murder attempt – which made him look like a total twerp. He should have known it was dangerous to sneak around a warehouse when a forklift was operating. It was the kind of thing that Jack would do.

Scott heard a buzz and swatted away a wasp. Soon he was being dive-bombed by an entire battalion.

'Looks like Scott still smells like a can of Cherry

98

Coke!' Jack laughed. His brother was prancing about, waving his arms in the air like a Bollywood dancer. His wet hair was standing on end and Emily's dad's baggy grey Rolling Stones t-shirt flapped in the breeze.

Normally Jack would have got his phone out and captured it all on video for later use, but he decided that he'd give Scott a break just this once. Almost getting flattened couldn't have been much fun.

And, on balance, Jack was glad he still had a *three-*dimensional brother.

—

It took a trip to Pirate Cove – a long swim, an hour of frisbee on the beach with Drift, a campfire (complete with sausages, eggs, beans and marshmallows) and beating Jack at rock-paper-scissors thirteen times in a row – before Scott mellowed out enough to discuss Operation Salamander again. But at last he was ready to listen to Jack and Emily's account of the secret meeting between Alesha Rahal and Shane Hazard.

'It was obvious neither of them was involved in stealing the Salamander,' Emily said.

'But what about this Rick Sullivan guy they were talking about?' Jack chimed in. 'He keeps trying to buy the Black Salamander.'

Scott looked up from the marshmallow toasting stick he was turning over the embers of the fire. '*The*

Rick Sullivan, you mean? The Irish computer games billionaire?'

Jack shrugged. 'I guess so. You'd have to be mega-loaded to afford to buy the Salamander.'

'Rick Sullivan collects iconic cars ... like the Lotuses and Aston Martins from the James Bond films,' Scott said. 'I remember reading about it somewhere. He keeps them all at his mansion near Dublin.'

Emily looked up from her notebook. 'So Sullivan has a motive. Silverwood Cars refused to sell the Salamander to him. Someone that rich is used to getting what they want. Perhaps he decided to just take it for himself!'

'But Alesha said he's in China,' Jack reminded her.

'He'd hardly do the dirty work himself, would he?' Scott pointed out. 'He probably employs people to blow his nose for him, let alone nick cars ... He'd pay someone. In fact, I bet he has an insider working for him at Wheel Power or at Silverwood Cars!'

Emily nodded, scribbling furiously. 'And he arranges for them to steal the Salamander while he's conveniently out of the country so he's not under suspicion! It all fits!'

Scott popped a perfect charred-on-the-outside-gooey-in-the-middle marshmallow into his mouth. He gazed out across the water. The sun was just beginning to sink in a sky the exact pink of the inside of the marshmallow.

As they put the fire out and got ready to row back

to The Lighthouse, Scott slipped his hand into his jeans pocket and felt the disc of crushed aluminium.

He'd decided to keep the Cherry Coke can as his lucky talisman.

Twelve

A Discovery at Pendragon Manor

Next morning Scott, Jack and Emily gathered round one of the three public computers in Castle Key library. Their mission was simple: to track down a connection between Rick Sullivan and anyone who worked at Silverwood Cars or the Wheel Power test track.

But although Rick Sullivan was a celebrity billionaire, when Scott entered his name into the search box along with SILVERWOOD or WHEEL POWER, no results popped up at all. Then he tried the names still on their suspect list: MONTY HOWARD, CONNOR JAMISON and ELIZABETH PRICE. They all drew a blank.

Jack yawned. Libraries always had that effect on him. He leaned across Scott and began punching in search terms almost at random: RICK SULLIVAN + SALAMANDER, AMPHIBIOUS, CORNWALL, CARRICKSTOWE, CASTLE KEY …

'*Bingo!*' he shouted, as a result popped up. He leaned back in his chair and punched the air with both fists. Then he smiled sheepishly at the librarian who'd come to investigate the disturbance. 'Gosh, I just love maths homework,' he said in his geekiest voice. 'I can't help getting a bit carried away sometimes!'

He turned back to the computer. Scott and Emily were gaping at the screen.

```
Computer games giant and well-known car
fanatic, Rick Sullivan, made a celebrity
guest appearance at the prestigious Classic
Car Collectors' Convention held at Pendragon
Manor, Castle Key, in May ...
```

The three friends grinned at each other. This could be the lead they'd been searching for. Sullivan had been right here in Castle Key – within a few miles of the

Wheel Power test track – only three months ago. Surely it couldn't be a coincidence!

'Hang on a minute!' Jack said as they left the library. 'I know it was *my* genius computer-searching skills that found that link with Castle Key, but if Sullivan was at Pendragon Manor back in May, how does that help us? He'd have needed a crystal ball to know that the Salamander would be coming to Wheel Power in three months' time ...'

Emily's face fell, but Scott shook his head. 'You don't just turn up at a test track on the off-chance you can have a quick spin in your priceless prototype supercar. It's probably all scheduled months in advance.' Suddenly he had an idea. 'I can check if you like!' He fished in his jeans pocket. Next to his lucky Cherry Coke can he found the autographed business card Will Stone had given him at the Grand Vista Hotel.

He called Stone's number and a few minutes later he had the information he wanted. 'I knew Will Stone would help us,' he told Jack and Emily. 'He was dead upset about the Black Salamander being stolen. He said it was booked in to be tested at Wheel Power over six months ago.'

Emily was delighted. 'Six months' notice! That's plenty of time for Rick Sullivan to have found out and planned the heist!' She climbed on her bike and Drift hopped into his basket. 'Let's go and see what we can dig up at Pendragon Manor.'

The sun was beating down from a clear blue sky as the friends cycled across South Moor, along the narrow winding road bordered by high verges splashed purple and pink, orange and yellow with wild flowers. At last they freewheeled down a steep hill and entered the deep shade of the ancient woods that encircled Pendragon Manor.

The grand Tudor mansion – with its gables and towers and jumble of huge chimneys sprouting from higgledy-piggledy roofs – was over four hundred years old. These days it was a venue for weddings and conferences, but it had a turbulent history – including its very own ghost. Emily glanced up at the tiny diamond-paned window under the eaves and couldn't help shuddering as she remembered hiding in the haunted attic during Operation Lost Star.

They propped their bikes against an old oak tree at the back of the house and climbed over the wall of the vegetable garden. They planned to enter through the kitchen door and find their friend, Vicky White. She usually worked in the kitchens at Pendragon Manor during her holidays from university and she was always happy to help Scott, Jack and Emily with their investigations; after all, she'd be in prison now if they hadn't cleared her name in their very first case together!

They were taking a short cut through the gooseberry

patch, when they were ambushed by a regal-looking lady in a pale blue suit. Her silvery-white hair, swept up in an elegant bun, matched the strands of pearls she wore over her blouse.

'Uh-oh!' Jack muttered under his breath. 'Bossy Bailey!' He'd encountered the housekeeper on more than one occasion and suspected they weren't exactly going to get the red carpet treatment.

Mrs Bailey jabbed the air with a small pair of scissors. 'What do you think you're doing rampaging through the soft fruit?'

'Hello, Mrs Bailey,' Scott said politely. 'We have a message for Vicky White. It's important.'

The housekeeper tutted. 'Deliver your message to Victoria quickly and then be on your way. I'm expecting a Health and Safety inspection today and I can't have a bunch of ragamuffins traipsing about the place. It's most unhygienic.'

Jack grinned. That explained why the housekeeper was lurking in the undergrowth with her scissors. She was snipping the thorns off the gooseberry bushes along the path in case they were a scratch hazard!

Suddenly Mrs Bailey caught sight of Drift snuffling around a compost bin. 'And *absolutely no animals* inside the house!'

'Of course!' Emily mumbled as they backed away.

Leaving Drift at the back door with a bowl of water, the friends entered through the old arched doorway.

They followed the delicious smell of baking along the cool stone corridor and peeped into the kitchen. Vicky was pulling a tray of fruit scones from a stainless steel oven the size of a spaceship. She saw the friends, smiled and came over to the door.

Jack helped himself to a scone. 'Just testing,' he mumbled with his mouth full. 'Don't want the Heath and Safety inspector getting food poisoning. Mmmm, yes, I think these should be safe.'

Vicky laughed. 'What can I do for you?'

Emily explained the quest to trace Rick Sullivan's activities during the classic car convention.

'I wasn't working here in May,' Vicky said, tucking her blonde fringe under her white catering cap. 'You could talk to Tony Goff, the parking valet. He looks after the guests' cars. Actually, you could get on Tony's good side by giving him a hand. Mrs Bailey's got him washing all the cars in the car park so that they're squeaky clean when the Health and Safety guy gets here!'

—

'Vicky didn't mention he was a giant,' Jack whispered as they spotted the huge man polishing a red Mini. When Scott called out rather nervously to ask if he was Tony Goff, Jack thought he might just roar, 'Fee fi fo fum!' by way of a reply.

Instead he rested his elbows on the roof of the car – he was wearing a sleeveless vest, showing off muscle-roped arms embellished with inky blue tattoos – and said, 'That's me!' in a perfectly friendly manner.

As Vicky had predicted, Tony Goff was grateful for the offer of help. He soon had Scott, Jack and Emily set up with cloths and buckets of soapy water. While Drift chased bubbles the friends worked hard, not just scrubbing, rinsing and polishing, but also steering the conversation around to the subject of Rick Sullivan.

'You must have had some cool cars here when that classic car convention was on,' Scott remarked.

Goff chatted enthusiastically about the makes and models that had turned up in the car park that week.

'I heard that billionaire guy, Rick Sullivan, was here,' Jack prompted. 'I bet *he* was driving an awesome car.'

'Too right! A classic Jaguar D-type. A real beauty! Not that I got much of a look in, mind you. Sullivan had his own staff with him – including his chauffeur. She was a trained mechanic, too, so she looked after the Jag.' Goff chuckled as he wiped away a spot of bird muck on the bonnet of a blue Mercedes. 'Funny, you don't see many female mechanics.'

Female mechanic? Jack stopped with his sponge halfway across the roof of a white Volvo. He hardly noticed the cold soapy water trickling into his armpits. He'd seen a female mechanic only the other day at the Wheel Power test track – *Elizabeth Price!* She had to be the link they'd been looking for. She'd worked for Rick Sullivan. Then she'd got the job at Wheel Power to help Sullivan steal the Black Salamander! And wasn't she the one who'd supposedly found the Black Salamander missing when she'd turned up for work at four o'clock in the morning? What could be more suspicious than that?

Emily had obviously had the same thought. 'Do you happen to know what Sullivan's chauffeur was called?' she asked casually.

Tony Goff thought for a moment. 'It began with a B. Betty? Bess? No, *Beth*. That's it! Beth Latimer.'

Thirteen

What's in a Name?

Tony Goff wrung out a sponge in his huge gnarly hands. 'Why are you so interested in Sullivan's chauffeur anyway?'

Jack, Scott and Emily stared at each other. *Beth Latimer?* They'd been so sure that Tony was going to say Rick Sullivan's chauffeur was called Elizabeth Price that, for once, even Emily was lost for words.

'Er, work experience!' Jack blurted eventually. Well,

it had worked on the receptionist when he'd bluffed his way into the press conference; he didn't see why it shouldn't work again now! 'Yeah, Emily wants to be a mechanic when she's older and she's looking for a female mechanic to do some work experience with.'

Tony smiled. 'Tell you what. I've got an old VW Beetle in the garage. You can come and help me strip the engine down when we've finished this one.'

Emily forced a smile and thanked him. She'd much rather spend the rest of the afternoon continuing her investigations. *But, when life gives you lemons*, she reminded herself, *make lemonade*. Knowing how to fix an engine was a skill that could come in very handy on a spy mission one day.

—

While Emily was being trained in the art of car mechanics, Scott and Jack wandered back towards the house. Jack was keen to taste-test some more scones in the kitchen, but Scott had other ideas.

'I bet Mrs Bailey keeps the contact details of everyone who stays here. Let's see whether any of the other suspects were here at the same time as Rick Sullivan.'

'And Bossy Bailey's just going to hand over the information?' Jack snorted. 'To a pair of unhygienic ragamuffins?'

Scott grinned. 'Who said anything about *asking*

her?' He pointed towards the front door. Mrs Bailey was bustling down the stone steps, between a pair of snooty-looking lion statues, to meet a grey-suited man with a briefcase and clipboard. The boys dodged out of sight behind the old yew maze on the lawn. They watched as the housekeeper ushered the man inside the house.

'That must be the Health and Safety inspector,' Scott said. 'Looks like Mrs B's going to be busy for a while. I'm sure she won't mind if we take a peek in her office.'

Jack stared at his brother. He couldn't have been more surprised if Scott had suggested base-jumping off the roof. Scott was meant to be the sensible one! 'Just to check she hasn't left any documents with sharp corners lying around,' Jack laughed. 'Someone could get a nasty paper cut.'

'We'd be doing her a favour really,' Scott agreed with a grin.

Moments later, Scott and Jack were peeping through the polished brass letterbox next to the front door. Mrs Bailey and the inspector were heading across the hall towards the kitchen corridor. As soon as they were out of sight, the boys crept in and stole across the vast entrance hall. The watchful eyes of assorted members of the Pendragon family gazed down on them from the gloomy old portraits that lined the wood-panelled walls.

Scott knew where the housekeeper's office was from

a previous mission: past the sweeping curved staircase and just along the main corridor. Jack stayed on guard outside the door while Scott slipped into the office.

It didn't take long to locate a filing cabinet labelled *Guest Details*. Scott flicked through until he found the date of the classic car convention in May. He glanced down the page and spotted Rick Sullivan's name. On the next line was written *Elizabeth Latimer*. He frowned at the name for a moment. Hadn't Tony Goff said that Sullivan's chauffeur was called *Beth* Latimer? But then he remembered a girl in his form at school called Beth Dalloway. She always hated it when substitute teachers who didn't know her read out her full name from the register: *Elizabeth* Dalloway. But before Scott could think about it any more, or look for more suspects' names, Jack opened the door a crack.

'Hurry!' he hissed. 'Someone's coming.'

Scott had his phone at the ready. He quickly photographed the page and stuffed it back in the file. He and Jack were tiptoeing back into the hall when they heard footsteps pelting towards them from the kitchen corridor. They ducked in next to a table in the alcove beneath the staircase.

Peeping out, they saw to their relief that the pelting person was Emily! Drift was racing along behind her, his claws clicking on the polished wooden floor. Emily looked wilder than ever, her hair flying out from a makeshift ponytail and oil daubed from head to foot like urban camouflage. Scott grabbed her as she sped past and pulled her into the alcove.

Emily struggled for a moment, almost knocking a vase of red roses off the antique table, before realizing her captor was only Scott. '*Marriage!*' she panted.

Scott rubbed his ribs where Emily had jabbed him with her pointy elbows. 'Marriage?' he echoed. He exchanged puzzled glances with Jack. True, they were standing under a banner that said *Timeless Romance: Choose Pendragon Manor for Your Perfect Wedding Venue*, but what did that have to do with anything?

'I was adjusting a carburettor,' Emily panted, 'when Tony got a phone call about the parking for a wedding next weekend. When he finished he said that it had reminded him that Rick Sullivan's chauffeur mentioned that she was going to be getting married soon – so, if I was trying to get in touch with her about work experience, she might have changed her name from Latimer ...'

'Fascinating!' Jack remarked sarcastically.

But Scott saw what Emily was getting at. 'Beth Latimer could be Elizabeth Price after all – if she married a man called Mr Price.'

'Exactly!' Emily breathed, clutching Scott by both arms in excitement.

Jack shook his head. Scott and Emily were gazing at each other with gleaming eyes across a vase of red roses under a sign saying *Timeless Romance*. If you didn't know they were talking about serious crime you'd think Scott had just proposed or something! 'Correct me if I'm wrong,' he said, 'but haven't you two geniuses missed a minor detail? Since when did women start changing their *first* names when they get married as well as their *sur*names?'

But Scott had already figured that one out. 'Beth is short for Elizabeth ...'

'I think we've found our insider!' Emily laughed, high-fiving with the boys and giving Drift a hug for good measure. 'Now that's what I call teamwork!'

Scott laughed. 'Now let's get out of here before Mrs Bailey finds our team and calls in Rentokil to exterminate us.'

The friends stepped out of the alcove into the hall.

Just in time to see the housekeeper and the Health and Safety inspector emerging from the kitchen corridor.

Fourteen

Escape!

The friends shrank back under the stairs.

Scott peeped out around the end of the staircase. Mrs Bailey and the Health and Safety inspector had stopped on the other side of the hall to examine a fire extinguisher. Scott looked round to tell the others to stay back. Suddenly his gut clenched in panic. They couldn't stay here! Attached to the wood panelling, about twenty centimetres behind Jack's head, was a small red fire extinguisher. If Mrs B was showing the inspector the fire safety measures, they'd be heading in this direction any second!

Scott knew he had to think of something fast. Emily looked like something that had just crawled out of an oily swamp. And then there was Drift! In her haste to find the boys and tell them about Beth Latimer's wedding, Emily had obviously forgotten that animals were strictly forbidden inside the house. And right now, Drift wasn't just your average forbidden animal; he was a rather whiffy forbidden animal with cobwebs and straw and grease matted into his fur from where he'd been exploring the outbuildings while Emily was working with Tony Goff.

They couldn't risk being seen.

If Pendragon Manor fails its inspection because of us, Scott thought, *Mrs Bailey will sue us for damages or have us locked up in the Tower of London – or both!*

Scott took another peek. The Health and Safety inspector was nodding and writing something on his clipboard. Mrs Bailey smiled and pointed towards the stairs. *Oh, no!* Scott thought. *If only we could disappear through a trapdoor or something …*

Of course! That was it!

They were standing right in front of the entrance to the secret tunnel that led to the middle of the maze! Scott remembered coming out through the hidden door under the stairs after being chased by an irate gardener during Operation Compass. If he could just find the concealed latch ...

Scott ran his hands over the polished wood panelling. At last he felt one of the panels give a little. He forced his fingernails under the edge of the join and tried to prise the door open, but it was no good. It wouldn't budge. Scott cursed under his breath as two of his fingernails broke. He needed something to use as a lever. He took his penknife out of his pocket, but with his broken nails he couldn't ease the blade out.

Suddenly Emily realized what he was doing. 'I've got a screwdriver!' she murmured, and began rummaging in her shoulder bag.

But there was no time. Scott could hear Mrs Bailey and the inspector's footsteps coming closer.

Jack patted his pockets. 'A coin would do it.' He grimaced. 'But I haven't got any!'

Scott closed his eyes and swallowed. Any moment, they would be discovered, cowering under the stairs like frightened mice. But just when it seemed they were done for, he had an idea.

His lucky talisman!

Scott whipped the crushed Cherry Coke can from his pocket and slid it into the crack in the panelling.

The little door flew open. Emily scooped Drift up and ducked through it. Shoving Jack ahead of him, Scott followed. He pulled the door shut behind them, willing it not to make a sound.

For several long moments the friends clung together in the dark, holding their breath and straining their ears for any noises on the other side of the door. At last, they breathed again. It seemed no one had seen them.

'That was a close one!' Emily murmured, pulling a torch from her bag.

The friends knew their way through the short tunnel that ran under the manor and the garden, and they were soon pushing open the creaky old trapdoor and climbing out into the heart of the maze. They flopped down on the grass and gazed up at the little square of blue sky between the towering yew hedges that surrounded them. Emily couldn't help giggling with relief. Jack laughed too, and then Scott, and suddenly they were all rolling around helpless with laughter. Drift joined in by springing about on top of them licking their faces.

Eventually Emily sat up. 'We'll have to go back to Wheel Power and follow Elizabeth Price,' she said when she got her breath back.

Scott agreed. 'If she's stolen the Black Salamander for Rick Sullivan she could have hidden it somewhere nearby until he gets back from China to pick it up. With luck she'll lead us to the hiding place.'

'It's Sunday afternoon,' Jack pointed out. 'She's probably not at work today.'

Emily sighed. 'If only we knew her home address.'

'Your wish is my command!' Scott took out his phone with a pantomime flourish and clicked on the photo he'd taken of the guest file in Mrs Bailey's office. He zoomed in and found the entry for Elizabeth Latimer. 'One address coming right up! Fifteen, Kenwyn Lane, Carrickstowe . . .'

Jack jumped up. 'What are we waiting for?' He held out a hand to pull Emily up. 'Now, who remembers their way out of the maze?'

They all looked at each other. There were five exits and that was just to get out of the centre. They'd been here before but they'd had a map that time!

Drift watched the friends for a moment. *You can always tell when humans are lost*, he thought. They started wandering around like confused squirrels. He could never understand why they didn't just use their noses! He headed for the third exit and sniffed the ground. Yes, this was it. He'd left a perfectly obvious scent mark last time they were here. He yipped once and wagged his tail.

'Look,' Emily cried. 'Drift knows the way!'

'Follow that nose!' Jack shouted.

'We're out of here!' Scott laughed.

And, before long, they were!

Kenwyn Lane was a narrow street of fishermen's cottages leading up a steep hill from the quay in the old part of Carrickstowe. The friends split up to watch number fifteen from different vantage points. Scott positioned himself behind a parked car at the top of the street, while Jack lurked outside a small café at the bottom.

Meanwhile, Emily and Drift climbed the cobbled alleyway that ran along the back of the cottages and crouched behind a group of dustbins. Hollyhocks and sunflowers burst out of tiny back gardens and terraces. Geraniums spilled from hanging baskets. Seagulls squawked at each other from the chimney pots.

It was almost an hour before Emily spotted Elizabeth Price coming out of her back door. She was wearing a t-shirt, denim shorts and flip-flops and her hair was wrapped in a towel. She had a pretty face with a sprinkle of freckles across her nose, but there were dark rings under her eyes. She pegged a load of washing onto the line to dry. Then she went back in. Emily made a note of the time. Half an hour later, Elizabeth Price came out again. She stroked a fat grey cat stretched along the top of a whitewashed wall. Then she went back in.

Emily was disappointed. A life of crime shouldn't be this boring! Maybe that's why Price had agreed to help Sullivan steal the Salamander, Emily mused. She'd be able to lead a more jet-setting lifestyle with the money he'd pay her ... but Emily's thoughts were interrupted by Elizabeth Price appearing again. This time she crossed the garden and headed down the alley. She'd taken the towel off and her blonde corkscrew curls bounced as she hurried down the slope. Emily and Drift followed.

Elizabeth Price didn't go far. She took a short cut through another alley, came out at the bottom of Kenwyn Lane and entered the café. She didn't notice Jack, who'd decided he needed to order something to maintain his cover, and was now sitting at a pavement table with a cheese toastie. Emily and Drift joined him. While Drift scouted for toast crumbs under the table, Emily quickly angled the parasol like a giant shield so they could peep round it to see in through the café window.

Elizabeth Price ordered a coffee. She sat down near the window. She stirred and sipped for a while. Then she stirred and sipped some more. Just when it seemed as though nothing would happen, she took out a pen and a piece of paper from her pocket. She rested the paper on a folded paper napkin and began to write a note. Emily craned her neck so far she almost dislocated her spine, but it was no good. Elizabeth kept her hand folded over the page as if afraid someone might copy her work.

'Probably just a shopping list,' Jack muttered.

'I don't think so,' Emily whispered. 'Look!'

Elizabeth Price had stood up. She'd left some change for a tip and hurried out without looking back.

She'd also folded the note in half and left it on the table.

Fifteen

The Secret Message

Emily knew exactly what she had to do: dash into the café, accidentally-on-purpose brush past the table, knocking the note to the floor, pick it up and sneak a look as she put it back. Simple!

At least it *would* have been simple if the man in the corner hadn't beaten her to it. He strolled past the table and, in one swift move, palmed the note and slipped it in his jeans pocket. Then he pushed open the door and left the café.

Emily and Jack ducked out of sight behind the parasol and watched the man walk down the lane towards the quayside. Emily had been so intent on observing Elizabeth Price she'd hardly noticed him at the corner table. Now she registered a middle-aged man with greying hair and the build of a retired boxer. Emily had seen photos of Rick Sullivan and, even from the back, she could tell this wasn't him. Sullivan was white for a start, and this guy was black.

'Come on,' Jack said. 'Let's follow him.'

Emily was about to agree when she had an idea. 'You go!' she said. 'I'll meet you back here.'

Emily flew into the café. To her dismay, the waitress was already clearing the place where Elizabeth Price had been sitting. Lunging at the table Emily grabbed the paper napkin, almost snatching it out of the startled woman's hand.

'Sorry!' Emily mumbled, clapping her hand over her face. 'Nosebleed!' Then she rushed out again.

When Scott came to find Jack at the café a few moments later, after giving up on his post at the top of the lane, he found Emily instead, sitting alone at a pavement table and staring at a white paper napkin as if it were a map of the lost city of Atlantis. He pulled up a chair.

Emily set the napkin back down, rested her cheek on the table and looked across the surface of the paper.

'I lost him!' Jack panted, running back up the hill to join them. 'He jumped in an old Volvo and drove off. I got the registration number though.' He held up a pencil and a scrap of paper with the number on.

Emily grunted but didn't lift her head from the table. 'Elizabeth Price was resting the paper on this napkin when she wrote the note,' she said. 'She was using a ballpoint pen so ...'

At last Scott realized what Emily was up to. 'So you can see the impression of the writing on the napkin!'

Emily nodded. 'But it's so faint I can hardly make it out. So far I've got *Me ... night ... lace ...*'

'Give it here!' Jack demanded. He began rubbing over the napkin with the side of the pencil point. As the napkin turned grey, faint white letters began to appear.

'Where did you learn that?' Emily laughed.

Jack grinned. 'I can't possibly reveal that information but let's just say it wasn't an official exam and I didn't steal the paper from Ruby McEllery's desk; it fell off. And I knew the answer anyway. I was just checking.'

Gradually the complete message was revealed. *Meet tonight at ten thirty. Same place. I'll be on foot.*

Emily found a roll of Sellotape in her bag, tore off a strip and stuck it over the message to preserve it before popping it into an evidence bag. They were so close to wrapping this case up she could almost *smell* victory. The man was clearly working for Rick Sullivan along with Price. He probably set the false trail for the police by taking the GPS tracker in the lorry to Plymouth, while Elizabeth drove the Black Salamander off and hid it somewhere. All they had to do was follow her tonight and she'd lead them to the hiding place. If she was going on foot it couldn't be far ...

'Let's meet here at ten,' Scott said. 'We'll watch for Elizabeth Price to leave her house.'

'Er, just one teensy problem with that!' Jack said, wiping his pencil-smudged hands on his shorts. 'I sort of signed up to do a whale-watch shift tonight.'

'You did *what*?' Scott demanded.

'It was when I was talking to Josie at the ice-cream van yesterday,' Jack said, attempting a breezy no-big-deal kind of voice. 'She said the whales are still in the channel. We're on the rota for ten o'clock.'

'*We're* on the rota?' Scott and Emily chorused in a perfect duet. Scott shook his head. 'Uh-uh! You're on your own.'

But Emily grinned. It was another of those lemon-and-lemonade moments. 'Jack's done us a favour. It gives us the perfect excuse to be out late at night. Mum and Dad won't mind if they know I'm out with the Nature Group. It's *educational*. We'll just do a tiny little detour to follow Elizabeth Price.'

'What about the whales?' Jack asked.

'That's *your* job,' Scott said.

'Why me?'

'Because you're the one who sold your soul to the

128

Nature Group for a double-scoop cornet,' Scott pointed out.

'It was a *triple* scoop, actually,' Jack muttered as they left the café.

—

It was always a challenge to move after one of Aunt Kate's Sunday roast dinners, complete with Yorkshire puddings, followed by apple pie and ice cream, but at nine o'clock the boys got on their bikes and set off across the island. Twilight was gathering fast; it was well into August now and the late-night sunsets of midsummer were already a thing of the past.

Emily and Drift were waiting for them in the hollow willow tree near the causeway. While Jack stomped off to North Point to report for whale-watching duty, taking Drift with him for company, Emily and Scott cycled over the causeway to Carrickstowe.

They parked their bikes near the quay and loitered outside the café on Kenwyn Lane. They were both dressed all in black with hoods pulled up to obscure their faces. *If a police officer sees us, we're in serious trouble*, Scott thought. *We couldn't look more like muggers if we tried!*

Just after ten, Elizabeth Price appeared from the alleyway at the back of the cottages. She'd tied her hair up in a scarf and put on a black tracksuit. She glanced left and right, then hurried down Kenwyn Lane.

Emily and Scott followed.

They tracked her across a park and through streets of houses until at last they were heading east out of Carrickstowe. Price marched along the grass verge, suddenly turning off into a road that doubled back towards the coast past a small industrial estate.

'There's nothing much down here,' Scott whispered. 'Apart from ...'

Emily finished his sentence. '... the Wheel Power test track!'

It was true. Elizabeth Price had almost reached the huge metal gates. Security lights beamed down like searchlights.

'They can't have hidden the Black Salamander here,' Scott murmured.

'Oldest trick in the book!' Emily whispered. 'Hide something in the last place people think to look – right under their noses.'

Elizabeth Price turned away from the gate and began jogging round the outside of the fence, skirting the compound and heading down a narrow track. The beam of her torch bounced in the dark as she ran. They were close to the sea now. Scott could hear it sighing like a huge animal breathing in its sleep. They crossed a small beach. Of course, Scott realized, Price was making for the private harbour that Wheel Power used for performance-testing boats.

Scott and Emily crouched behind a low brick wall

and watched as their target stopped again, blocked by another fence. She stood looking up at a security camera. Scott noticed it was much older and clunkier than the ones in the main part of the compound. It rotated slowly on its mounting, scanning the area near a small gate. As the camera turned away, Price darted across to the gate, punched a number into the keypad, shot through to the other side and ran on.

'Smooth,' Emily whispered admiringly.

'Keypad,' Scott groaned. 'We can't get through to the harbour without a code.'

But Emily had an idea. She had a good memory for numbers and hadn't forgotten the six-digit code Alesha Rahal had given her for her office door. It might not work for this gate, of course, but it was worth a try.

Mimicking Elizabeth Price's movements, Emily waited for the camera to begin to swing away. She scurried across the pool of light to the gate. She hesitated for a moment, checking the position of numbers she needed, but before she could press the first one, she heard Scott's anxious call.

'Get back!'

She dived back into the shadows out of the scope of the camera.

'You were too slow,' Scott said. 'The camera was already moving back. It would have caught you.'

Emily sighed with frustration. 'OK, I'll do it faster

this time.' Then she told Scott the code. 'If it works you'll have to do the same.'

Emily waited for her moment again, then sprinted to the gate. This time she was quicker. She jabbed in the six numbers, holding her breath, dreading the wail of security alarms. Nothing happened. Then there was a soft click. Her heart in her mouth, Emily pushed the gate. It opened on silent hinges. She was in!

She scurried for cover behind an upside-down speedboat that had been pulled out of the water for repairs. Moments later she was joined by Scott.

Looking out from behind the hull, Scott scanned the small harbour. It was roughly built from stone blocks and curved round to end in a long jetty. Several boats were moored up and bobbed gently on their ropes. There were ramps and pulleys and a small crane for lifting the boats in and out of the water. The only light came from a crescent moon. Wisps of cloud turned from black to silver as they drifted past.

At first Scott couldn't see Elizabeth Price. Then he spotted a red dot moving about in the dark like a laser pointer. A whiff of cigarette smoke mingled with the smell of boat oil and wet rope. He heard a soft clunk and looked back to the gate. Emily's tightening grip on his arm told him she'd heard it too. Price's accomplice was letting himself in. She must have given him her security code. Was this how they had broken in to steal the Black Salamander in the first place?

Elizabeth Price walked back along the harbour and met a man halfway. They began talking. But Emily could only catch a few words: *security systems ... getaway route ...*

'Rick Sullivan will pay ...' Price said, but the rest of her sentence and the man's reply were lost beneath the whine of a motorbike on a distant road.

Emily ground her teeth. She was so close to solving the case! But she had to get closer if she wanted to find out where the Black Salamander was hidden. Before Scott could stop her she shucked her bag off her shoulder, broke away from the upturned boat and crawled along the harbour on her hands and knees. She'd almost reached the cover of a small crane when her knee knocked a stone into the water.

Elizabeth Price and the man fell silent.

'There's someone there!' the man said.

Behind the boat Scott felt the fear rise in his throat. This guy had been paid by one of the richest men on the planet to steal one of the most expensive cars in the world. He wasn't going to muck about. *If he finds us he'll tread on us like ants*, he thought.

'Probably just a cat,' Price answered.

'Cats don't say *ouch*!' The man switched on a torch and directed its powerful beam at Emily.

Or at least at the spot where Emily had been a moment before.

Sixteen

Over the Edge

The man swept the torch beam from side to side. There was no sign of Emily.

Scott didn't know what to do. Instinct told him to run out from behind the boat and search for her. She could have been seriously injured or fallen in the water. But then his brain butted in – he'd have heard a scream or a splash. And if she'd somehow managed to hide, he'd just end up blowing her cover.

Price and the man with the torch were coming closer. Scott had to make a decision and make it fast.

He slid his lucky talisman from his pocket and ran his thumb over the crushed metal. Then he took his phone from his other pocket and keyed in a number.

As soon as he heard the words, 'Carrickstowe Police, how can I help you?' he hurled the Cherry Coke can along the harbour. It soared like a miniature frisbee, bounced off the crane and clattered to the ground.

While Elizabeth Price and the man ran off to investigate the noise, Scott whispered urgently into the phone, 'The harbour behind the Wheel Power test track. Emergency!'

Then he ran to the place where Emily had disappeared. Where was she? Suddenly he heard a disembodied voice.

'Down here!'

Scott looked down past his trainers and over the edge. There was nothing there. Then, as the clouds shifted, he saw Emily's face looking up at him, pale and luminous in the moonlight. He knelt and looked closer. She was clinging to the harbour wall, holding onto a rope with one hand and a metal mooring ring with the other. Her legs were dangling in the water. 'Quick,' she hissed. 'Come on!'

Scott heard footsteps behind him. He had no choice

but to grab a rope and lower himself over the edge. He gasped as the cold water swallowed him up to the waist.

Their noses pressed against the damp slimy wall, Scott and Emily clung on like a pair of barnacles. Time passed. Very slowly.

'I can't hold on much longer,' Emily whispered.

Scott reached across so she could grip onto his shoulder, even though his own arm muscles were about to snap like elastic bands. 'I can't hear anything,' he said after what seemed like several hours. 'They must have left.'

Using their last shreds of strength, Emily and Scott hauled themselves up until they could peep over the edge.

Straight into the dazzling light of a high-powered torch beam!

Blinking against the glare they saw two faces looking down at them, one pale with blonde curls tied up in a scarf, one dark with short greying hair.

'Hey! I saw these kids hanging around the café earlier!' the man yelled. 'Get up here! I want to know what you're up to.'

But at that moment another voice boomed into the night. 'And I'd like to know what *you're* up to!'

Scott was so relieved he almost fell back into the water.

He knew that voice. It was deep and dignified with

the trace of a Middle Eastern accent. And it belonged to Detective Inspector Hassan.

'Arrest those two!' Emily shouted. 'They stole the Black Salamander!'

—

Meanwhile Jack was having a much less eventful time at North Point. The orcas had clearly decided to cancel their evening performance. The most exciting thing that had happened was Don Penrose, the boss of the Nature Watch Group, turning up with a flask of lukewarm tea.

A whole hour of my life I'll never get back! Jack thought. *If I'd wanted to be this bored, I could have stayed at home and watched* Politics Tonight *on Aunt Kate's black and white TV.*

Drift wandered off over the scrubby sand dunes towards some tumbledown boat sheds. He trailed back, whimpering softly. Then he looked out to sea and howled.

Even Drift's bored, Jack thought. *He's wishing he'd gone with Emily!*

Don Penrose droned on about orca populations and migration routes and about the 'whale-cams' the group had set up to film the whales underwater. 'Just down there!' he said proudly, pointing to a platform a little way out from the shore.

Jack gazed across the water to the black mass of the mainland. The lights of Carrickstowe twinkled invitingly as if taunting him. Somewhere over there, Emily and Scott were having an epic adventure and solving the mystery without him.

It was so unfair!

Penrose followed Jack's gaze. 'Trouble is,' he said, stroking his unruly beard, 'we keep getting crank calls from people saying they've spotted the orcas. One old chap rang to say he'd seen the whales while he was walking his dog over on the mainland the other night – but he described a pair of giant shark fins, nothing like orca fins at all! Another lady thought she'd seen the Loch Ness monster in Keyhole Cove!' He shook his head in amusement and offered Jack a biscuit from a Tupperware container.

Jack was about to take one when he saw they were all digestives – the only kind of biscuit he didn't like!

And just when he thought the evening couldn't get any worse, he sat on a wasp.

—

'A private investigator?' Scott groaned. 'I don't believe it!'

Scott and Emily were sitting in the back of a police car with blankets wrapped round them.

Emily shivered miserably. She'd got it all wrong!

There'd been no arrests. As soon as the police had arrived, the man had given D. I. Hassan his card.

'*Miles Chapman*,' D. I. Hassan read out. '*Chapman Private Investigations.*'

Chapman nodded. 'I do missing persons mostly, divorce cases, that kind of thing, so when I got a call from Miss Price here, asking me to help track down a missing supercar for Rick Sullivan, it was an offer I couldn't refuse. We came down here to check out possible routes in and out of the compound.'

Elizabeth Price pulled off her headscarf and smiled at D. I. Hassan. 'It's true,' she said. 'I was Rick Sullivan's chauffeur up till a couple of months ago, but I took the job at Wheel Power when I got married because I didn't want to be travelling so much. When Rick heard that the Black Salamander had disappeared he was gutted. He was still hoping that Silverwood might sell it to him after they'd finished the Hollywood filming. He asked me to see what I could find out about where it had gone.' Elizabeth made an apologetic face at D. I. Hassan. 'No offence, but Rick felt that the police were getting nowhere fast ...'

At that point one of the other police officers looked up from her radio and addressed D. I. Hassan. 'Chapman's story all checks out, sir. Private investigator, registered in Exeter.'

'But why were you sneaking around in the dark if you weren't doing anything wrong?' Emily couldn't help asking through chattering teeth as she was bundled into the police car.

Elizabeth Price shrugged. 'I knew the police wouldn't take kindly to people interfering with their investigations.'

D. I. Hassan directed a meaningful look at Emily. 'Quite right!'

'And I had to keep the whole thing secret from my husband so as not to worry him,' Price went on. 'He thought I'd get into trouble if I got involved.' She pressed her lips into a wry smile. 'I guess I should have listened to him.'

—

Emily climbed into bed. Drift curled up on her knees.

'Well, it wasn't a *total* disaster,' she told him.

Drift twitched one ear to show he was listening.

'We've eliminated another suspect.' Emily crossed Elizabeth Price's name off the list. 'And there was something else,' she said sleepily. 'I found some *lemonade* in the police car ...'

Drift snuffled. Being a dog, he didn't know what lemonade was, of course! Even if he did, it wouldn't have helped. This wasn't real lemonade. It was metaphorical lemonade, the make-the-best-of-a-bad-situation kind.

While she'd been shivering under the blanket in the

police car Emily had noticed a folder. It was lying open on the back seat right next to her.

Which meant Emily simply couldn't *help* noticing the photocopy of a speeding ticket made out to Frank Evans.

'When life gives you lemons ...' Emily murmured as she fell asleep.

Seventeen

Emily Figures it Out

Next morning the boys trudged to The Lighthouse to meet Emily. For Jack, every step was a painful reminder of the unfortunately placed wasp sting.

'Totally unprovoked attack!' he grumbled. 'If humans went round stabbing people in the bum we'd be locked up for Grievous Bodily Harm!'

'It wasn't unprovoked!' Scott snapped. 'You *sat* on it!' Scott had his own problems this morning. Hanging around up to his waist in cold water had left him with a nasty cold.

They expected to find Emily fed up and fuming about last night's fiasco. But, to their surprise, she was sitting in the dining room surrounded by maps, timetables, print-outs and scribbled notes. She looked up and smiled in a bright busy-but-friendly-teacher kind of way as they entered the sunny room built onto the side of the lighthouse tower. 'Aha! There you are. Just in time!'

'In time for what?' Scott asked warily, wiping his dripping nose on a scrap of tissue.

'I've worked out how he did it!'

'How who did what?' Jack helped himself to a plate of leftover croissants from the sideboard and sat down.

Emily thrust a piece of paper in Scott's direction.

'It's a speeding ticket,' Scott said, squinting at the blurry photo of an official document.

Jack grabbed the paper out of his hand. 'It's made out to Frank Evans. Where did you get this?'

'It was in D. I. Hasssan's car last night,' Emily said. 'I took a picture on my phone and printed it out.'

Jack reached for another croissant. 'So old Frankie's a bit of a boy racer. He was doing eighty miles an hour on the A30. So what?'

Emily sighed. 'Look at the date.'

Scott swallowed. He felt as if a hedgehog had taken up residence in his throat. 'August twentieth,' he read out.

'Which just happens to be the night the Black Salamander was stolen!' Emily said.

'What's the big deal?' Jack asked. 'We know Frank Evans was delivering hubcaps to the factory in Weymouth that night. The A30 is on the way to Weymouth, isn't it?'

Emily could hardly contain her impatience. 'Look at the time on the ticket.'

Jack took a look. 'Ten past seven in the evening.'

'Exactly! That's far too early! I've looked it up on Dad's road maps.' Emily swept her hand over the pile of maps on the table. 'It takes about four hours to drive from Carrickstowe to Weymouth. Frank Evans didn't make the delivery to the Auto-Dynamic factory until five o'clock in the morning. So even if he was crawling along, which he obviously wasn't' – Emily pointed at the speeding ticket – 'he wouldn't have needed to set out until *well after midnight*.' She looked at the boys with a triumphant gleam in her dark eyes.

'So what are you saying?' Jack asked.

Emily leaned back in her chair. She *lived* for moments like these: explaining her brilliant deductions to an admiring audience, just like a modern-day Sherlock Holmes. She resisted the temptation to kick off with *Elementary, my dear Watson*. 'We know from the CCTV cameras that a lorry left the Wheel Power test track shortly after midnight and was then seen driving onto a ferry in Plymouth a couple of hours later. We're supposed to think that the Black Salamander was on board because its secret GPS tracker was sending back signals from the lorry, but according to our theory *it's just the tracker* from the Salamander that was on that lorry, not the car itself ...'

'Yeah, yeah, we know this,' Jack grumbled.

Emily took no notice. 'I think Frank Evans was driving that lorry!' she said dramatically. 'He could have taken the hubcaps with him. When he got to Plymouth, he handed the lorry over to an accomplice who drove it onto the ferry while he continued on to Weymouth to make the delivery to Auto-Dynamic.' Emily paused and tapped one of the maps. 'It's about two and a half hours from Plymouth to Weymouth – so he could have just about made it by five in the morning.'

'But how did he get from Plymouth to Weymouth if he'd handed over the lorry?' Scott asked.

Jack waved a croissant at him. 'Simple! He hired a van at the ferry terminal.' He grinned at Emily. 'Am I right or am I right?'

Scott sniffed into his tissue. *Is it physically possible to drown in snot?* he wondered. 'But we know he *wasn't* in a hire vehicle. Em said that the guy at Auto-Dynamic told her Frank was definitely driving a Wheel Power delivery van.'

Emily beamed at Scott as if he were her star pupil. 'Well remembered! That was the part that had me stumped at first, too.'

Suddenly Jack saw why the time on the speeding ticket was so important. Croissant crumbs spurted across the table. 'He drove the Wheel Power delivery van to Plymouth earlier in the evening,' he blurted, 'and left it in the ferry terminal car park, ready to use later so he could drive to Auto-Dynamic!'

'Exactly,' Emily said. 'He could easily have got the train back from Plymouth to Carrickstowe. I've checked the timetable. There's a train that leaves Plymouth at eight-thirty-five. It's a bit slow but it would have got Frank back to Carrickstowe at ten-thirty. Plenty of time for him to drive the lorry out of Wheel Power so it could be seen on camera leaving at quarter past midnight, drive it up to Plymouth with the GPS tracker on board and hand it over to somebody else! Meanwhile an accomplice drives the Salamander – minus its tracking devices – off to the unknown hideout! And, of course, Frank Evans gives himself an alibi by supposedly being miles away in Weymouth.'

'Wow!' Jack whistled. 'That's genius!'

Emily grinned. 'Thanks!'

'I meant *Old Frankie*'s a genius,' Jack laughed. 'Coming up with that crafty scheme.' He noticed Emily's grin start to fade. 'Oh, alright, you're a genius too, for figuring it out!'

'It's all still just a theory though, isn't it?' Scott said.

'It would explain why he looked so shattered the next morning,' Jack laughed, remembering the moment when he'd been hiding in the car park during his solo mission to the press conference. Frank Evans had pulled up in the delivery van, yawning and with a cup of coffee in his hand. 'He must have been driving all night and only just made it back in time for work.'

They all looked up as Emily's mum hurried in with a tray of cutlery to set up the tables for lunch. 'Em, I asked you to start clearing away the guests' breakfast buffet an hour ago,' she said.

Emily looked around at the plates and cups she'd shoved to one end of the table as if seeing them for the first time. 'Sorry, Mum, I'll do it in a minute. Jack and Scott will help.'

Jack winced. 'Ooh, I'm not sure I'm up to it. Wasp sting! Very painful.'

'I can't believe the guests ate *all* those croissants,' Maria Wild murmured as she bustled out.

Jack grinned at Scott and Emily. 'So, let's call the police and tell them we've solved the case. It was Frank Evans all along. No wonder he was trying to frighten us off with his forklift!'

Emily hesitated. 'Like Scott said, it's still only a theory. We need more evidence. And we need to find out who Evans was working with. Someone must have driven the Salamander away and hidden it while he was taking the GPS to Plymouth in the lorry.'

'We've ruled out almost everyone else at Wheel Power …' Jack pointed out. 'There's only Monty Howard, the chief engineer, and Connor Jamison, the driver, left on the suspect list.'

'I'll see if I can dig up anything about Frank Evans,' Scott volunteered. 'He might have criminal connections or something.'

Jack laughed. 'You mean *Crusher* Evans, your arch-enemy!'

Scott rolled his eyes, but Jack's comment was nearer the truth than he liked to admit. This time it was personal!

Emily nodded. 'Good idea. And I'll pay Elizabeth Price a visit. She's been trying to solve this case as well. Maybe I can persuade her to share her findings with us – like whether Connor Jamison and Monty Howard have alibis for the night of the theft.'

'Good luck with that!' Jack said sarcastically. 'After you and Scott grassed her up to the police, I'm sure she'd *love* to help you out.'

Emily swatted him with her notebook. 'Just you wait and see! What are *you* going to do?'

Jack made a pathetic face. 'I'm on sick leave! Do you think it's possible to sue wasps for personal injury?'

Scott got up to leave. 'In that case, you'll have time to clear the tables while Emily and I get to work. Come on, Em!'

'No way!' Jack spluttered. But he was talking to himself!

Even Drift had deserted him.

Eighteen

Further Enquiries

'Here goes,' Emily murmured to Drift as she knocked on the door of number fifteen, Kenwyn Lane. She knew Jack was right. After last night, Elizabeth Price wasn't likely to welcome her as her new best friend.

Elizabeth opened the door, wiping her hands on a tea towel. 'Oh, it's you!' she said crossly.

'Who's that, love?' The voice came from inside the cottage.

'Nobody!' Elizabeth called over her shoulder. She turned back to Emily. 'What do you want?'

'Just to talk to you for a minute.'

'I'm listening.'

Emily looked down at her feet. 'I'm sorry. We didn't mean to mess up your investigation.'

'What were you doing at the Wheel Power harbour anyway?'

'Same as you,' Emily said. 'We're investigating the case of the Black Salamander.'

'You'd better come in,' Elizabeth sighed. Emily followed her into a small living room decorated in shades of duck-egg blue and cream.

'This is my husband, Ian,' Elizabeth said, smiling in the direction of a dark-haired, handsome young man watching snooker on a widescreen TV.

Emily said hello. Drift trotted over and parked himself at the man's side, nuzzling his hand in a friendly greeting.

Elizabeth showed Emily through to a small kitchen at the back of the cottage. 'We can talk in here.'

Vegetables and pasta had been set out on the counter. 'You're making spaghetti bolognese,' Emily guessed. 'I'll help chop,' she offered, picking up a knife. 'I hope you didn't get into too much trouble with the police last night.'

Elizabeth Price poured water into a saucepan and lit the gas. 'Well, I got a long lecture from Detective

Inspector Hassan about leaving the police to do their job.'

'Oh, yeah, I get that one all the time!' Emily said with a grin.

Elizabeth smiled and threw Emily an apron. 'So, where've you got to in your investigation?' She paused. 'And call me Beth, by the way. Elizabeth's way too formal.'

Emily explained her theory about the GPS tracker being removed and driven to Plymouth on the lorry by Frank Evans – while his accomplice hid the Salamander.

Beth nodded thoughtfully as she stirred vegetables into the sauce. 'So who do you think was working with Evans?'

Emily took her notebook from her bag and ran through the suspect list. 'We've ruled out Will Stone, because he was in Birmingham with his wife having a baby. And Alesha Rahal and Shane Hazard clearly had nothing to do with it. And now we've ruled you out too, of course!'

Beth raised her eyebrows. 'Wow! Good work! I should have hired you instead of Miles Chapman.'

Emily glowed with pride.

'Something smells good!' Ian Price called from the living room.

Beth put her head round the door and then turned back to Emily with a smile. 'Ian has MS – multiple sclerosis – and he gets a lot of pain. He was having a bad day today, but your dog has really cheered him up.'

Emily glowed with even greater pride. Drift was a very special dog! 'Connor Jamison and Monty Howard are the only suspects left on my list,' she said, eager to get back to the case. 'I wondered, do you have any intelligence on those two that you'd be prepared to share? Do they have alibis for the night the Salamander was stolen?'

Beth reached a folder down from a shelf above the cookbooks. 'Monty Howard was staying at a small hotel in Carrickstowe. He had dinner there at seven. That was confirmed by one of the waiters. He said he then went for a walk and was back in his room by ten.'

'Did anyone see him?' Emily asked.

'We have a couple of sightings on the seafront at about nine, but nothing after that.'

'What about Connor Jamison?' Emily queried.

Beth grinned. 'He was out partying all night!'

'In Carrickstowe?' Emily laughed. Carrickstowe wasn't exactly famous for its celebrity nightlife.

'At Trewidden Hall,' Beth explained. 'Do you know it?'

Emily nodded. She'd been to the stately home just north of Carrickstowe on a school trip. She knew it had been the home of the wealthy Huddlestone family for generations.

'Connor Jamison's girlfriend is Miffy Huddlestone – the famous model,' Lisa said. 'She's a distant cousin of the Trewidden Huddlestones. The party was to launch her new designer perfume.' She slid the latest copy of *Hello* magazine along the counter. Emily flicked through pictures of Connor Jamison grinning over a glass of champagne, his arm around a glamorous dark-haired woman in a sequinned dress.

'He could have sneaked out for a while,' Emily suggested.

'His car was parked at Trewidden Hall all night. And I've spoken to several people who were at the party. They all say he was pretty drunk. I'm not sure he *could* have driven the Salamander away even if he'd wanted to!'

Emily sighed. 'Yeah, and why *would* he have wanted to anyway? Without the Black Salamander, Connor doesn't get to go to the Monaco Motor Show or do the stunt driving in Hollywood. Same for Monty Howard. Why would he steal the car he designed himself?'

'Exactly,' Beth said. 'Neither of them has a motive.' She paused while she drained the pasta. 'Would you like to stay for lunch?'

Emily accepted. The spaghetti bolognese *did* smell good.

And she couldn't wait to tell Jack how wrong he'd been!

Meanwhile, Scott was in the library scrolling through old copies of the *Birmingham Post* on the computer.

He'd racked his brains for ways to try to find out more about Frank Evans. Stuck for ideas, he'd finally emailed Will Stone. It had turned out to be an inspired move! Will phoned back as soon as he received the message. He was taking care of his new baby, Chloe, while his wife had a nap. He was pushing the pram up and down the garden as he spoke.

'What do I know about Frank Evans?' Will repeated. 'Well, he used to work at Silverwood Cars but he left a few years before I started working there. I don't know what happened exactly, but I heard rumours he was sacked for some reason. I think he took Silverwood to court over it.'

A piercing cry cut across Will's words. Scott held the phone away from his ear.

'Sorry, I've got to go,' Will Stone sighed. 'I wish babies came with a manual – like a car!'

Scott laughed and thanked him. He took the crushed Cherry Coke can out of his pocket and turned it over in his palm. It had been worth running back down to the harbour to retrieve it last night. His talisman had brought him luck again. If there'd been a court case, the story would have made the newspapers.

All he had to do was find it!

He didn't have much to go on, though. He didn't even know the year. But just when Scott thought it was a hopeless quest, the headline popped up on the screen. SILVERWOOD WINS CASE AGAINST EVANS. Forgetting all about his drippy nose and scratchy throat, he scanned the story.

Frank Evans (38) was fired from his position as Computer Officer at Silverwood Cars. Silverwood bosses claim Evans was ordering extra computer equipment through the company to sell for his own profit. Evans has always denied any wrongdoing.

Oh, yeah! Got you! Scott thought. OK, so sneaking a few extra printers and laptops through the accounts wasn't exactly the crime of the century, but it meant Frank Evans had a grudge against Silverwood Cars for sacking him! It was a perfect motive! He wanted to get back at them by stealing their prized new supercar.

And there was something else about the story that was also significant. Evans hadn't always been a forklift driver – he used to work with computers. That meant he might well have had the skills to reprogram the security systems at Wheel Power so that the alarms didn't go off.

It was a double whammy!

Scott printed out the article, ran out of the library and phoned Emily to share the news.

'Of course!' Emily shouted. 'It all makes sense!' She was on her way back from Beth Price's house and had stopped halfway across the causeway when her phone rang. She leaned her bike against the wall and gazed out across the sparkling waves towards North Point as she spoke. The rocks were deserted. It seemed the Nature Watch Group had given up on the whales.

'Remember when all the alarms went off the first time we visited the test track?' Scott went on. 'The guard told us Frank had accidentally "mistyped his code" into the keypad. That could have been when he was tampering with the system.'

'And Frank could easily have drugged the guard,' Emily added. 'He just had to put sleeping pills in the coffee at the vending machine ...'

'Did you get any information from Elizabeth Price?' Scott asked.

Emily explained that Connor Jamison had an alibi. 'And Monty Howard was on his own for most of the evening,' she said, 'but I really can't see him being Frank Evans' partner in crime.'

Scott agreed. 'I've been thinking,' he said. 'We're running out of suspects. Maybe Evans was working alone.'

'But *someone* must have driven the Salamander away while Frank took the GPS tracker on the lorry to Plymouth,' Emily pointed out.

'Not if the police were right all along,' Scott said. 'Perhaps Frank just loaded the Black Salamander onto the lorry and drove it to Plymouth without taking the secret GPS tracker out.'

Emily hated to admit that her lovely theory could be wrong, but she had to agree it was starting to look that way. In which case, the Salamander really had been taken on a ferry to Europe and they had no hope of finding it.

She cycled the rest of the way home in a cloud of gloom.

—

When Scott got back to Stone Cottage he found Jack sprawling on the sofa in his dressing gown. Boomerang, the kitten, was draped across his knees. They were watching a horror film together while Jack worked his way through a plate of chocolate brownies. 'They're medicinal,' Jack explained. 'Got to build up my strength after that wasp sting.'

Scott sniffed. He took a brownie and flopped down in an armchair.

Aunt Kate came in and handed him a mug. 'Hot honey, lemon and ginger,' she said. 'It'll soon see that cold off.' Scott thanked her, blew away the steam and took a sip.

'I got you a present,' Jack lobbed a box of tissues in Scott's direction. 'Don't say I never give you anything!'

'Cheers!' Scott was quite touched that his brother had done something nice for once. But not for long! 'Ha! Ha!' he groaned as he opened the pack and saw the tissues were printed with pink flowers and fairies! He took one and blew his nose with extra noisy gurgling sound effects, drowning out the zombie invasion on the TV.

Jack threw a cushion at him. 'Euggh! That's gross!' he laughed. 'So how did you two ace investigators get on this afternoon?' he added.

Scott updated Jack with the new information. 'I'm starting to think Frank Evans was working alone,' he concluded. 'Looks like he took the Black Salamander to Plymouth on the back of the lorry after all.'

Jack dragged his eyes away from the TV, where a particularly gruesome zombie versus alien skirmish was taking place. 'I know you want to pin the whole thing on Frank Evans because he nearly flattened you,' he said. 'But there's no way the Black Salamander was on the back of that lorry. I've got proof!'

Nineteen

Brainwaves All Round

'Proof?' Scott spluttered, almost choking on the hot lemon drink. 'What *proof*?'

Jack handed him his phone. The screen showed a photo of a white lorry driving up Castle Key High Street. 'Nearly knocked me off my bike when I was on my way to the chemist for some wasp-sting ointment,' Jack said. 'It's the same kind of lorry that was seen leaving Wheel Power on the night of the theft.'

Scott rolled his eyes. 'It's hardly likely to be the same lorry! There must be thousands of these on the road.'

'Do I *look* like I'm stupid or something?' Jack snorted.

Scott resisted the temptation to answer.

'Of course I know it's not the same lorry! But look how low it's sitting on its axles. That shows it's fully loaded. The lorry that was caught on camera at the test track was much higher on its axles. I know because I saw it on the CCTV video footage at the press conference …' Jack paused for a moment to make the most of the stunned expression on Scott's face. 'Which proves it couldn't have been carrying a massive great weight like the Black Salamander!'

Scott stared at his brother in astonishment. How could someone who spent so much time acting so dumb suddenly come up with something so smart?

When the friends met for breakfast at Dotty's Tea Rooms on the seafront the next morning, Emily was delighted with Jack's amazing observation skills.

'That's brilliant!' she said. 'The Salamander can't have been in the lorry, after all!' She took a bite of her pancake. 'We *were* right about the Salamander being taken out of the compound some other way. The question is, how?'

Jack poured maple syrup over the mountain of strawberry waffles he'd treated himself to as a reward for his utterly braintastic stroke of genius. 'It's vanished into thin air! It *has* got active camouflage, you know!'

'But Monty Howard told us the technology wasn't good enough yet for the Salamander to be invisible when it's moving,' Scott pointed out. 'So how did it get past all the security cameras ...' Suddenly he broke off, staring at his bacon sandwich as if in a trance.

'You OK?' Emily asked. 'Is your cold still bothering you?'

Scott shook his head. His cold was almost gone. He felt much better. In fact, he'd just had a brainwave so spectacularly monumental that it made Jack's lorry observation look like one plus one equals two. 'The Salamander didn't vanish into thin air!' he murmured. 'It vanished into thin *water*!'

Emily and Jack stared at him.

Scott looked up. 'When we were at the harbour I noticed that there weren't many cameras round the back of the Wheel Power compound – and they were pretty old ones, too. They probably take a series of still pictures instead of video footage. Which means they might fail to pick up a car driving past slowly with active camo on ...' He grabbed a sugar cube and a knife and held them over his banana milkshake. 'The thief could have driven the Salamander down the track at the back of the compound, onto the harbour, down the boat ramp and into the sea.' Scott let go of the sugar cube. It slid down the knife and plopped into the milkshake. 'All without being seen!'

Emily nodded. 'Of course!'

'But they *were* seen!' Jack shouted all of a sudden. '*Shark fins!*'

'Shark fins?' Scott and Emily echoed in unison.

'When I was on whale-watch duty, Don Penrose told me an old man on the mainland had reported seeing the orcas late at night. But they didn't take this guy seriously because he said he saw two massive shark fins. The dorsal fins of orcas are long and curved.'

'The Black Salamander has two triangular fins that flip up at the back when it goes underwater,' Emily cried. '*That's* what the man saw!'

Scott dragged his hands through his hair. The pieces were starting to fall into place. And he'd just remembered something else that Monty had told them about the Black Salamander's underwater performance: it could only stay submerged for about twenty minutes before the air supply ran out. 'They can't have taken it very far ...' he murmured. 'Only a mile or two ...'

Suddenly Emily was on her feet making 'Ooh, ooh!' noises. The boys recognized this manic monkey impression – it meant she was too excited to get the words out. 'It's right here!' she spluttered eventually.

Jack pretended to look under the tablecloth. 'Where?'

'On Castle Key,' Emily laughed. 'It's only a mile

across the channel. They could have made it here easily.'

Scott nodded excitedly. He remembered looking across the channel from the Wheel Power harbour towards Castle Key island. There were almost no lights. The coast around North Point was deserted. It would be the perfect place to land without being seen ...

Jack could feel another brainwave bubbling up. 'So, does that active camouflage work underwater?' he asked slowly.

Scott shrugged. 'I don't know. But why would you bother? It's not like there are underwater CCTV cameras to keep an eye on antisocial fish!'

Jack grinned mysteriously. He'd just remembered something else Don Penrose had told him on the night of the whale-watch, in between the digestive biscuits and the wasp sting.

He told Scott and Emily about the whale-cam the Nature Watch Group had installed on the underwater platform to try to film the orcas.

The three friends looked at each other, eyes shining with excitement. 'Now we just have to find Don Penrose,' Scott said.

'Hang on!' Emily rummaged in her bag and fished out the leaflet they'd been given when they joined the Nature Watch Group. She turned to the diary of events. 'Don Penrose is giving a talk on the Shrews of Cornwall at the village hall this morning ...'

'What time?' Jack asked.

'Ten-thirty.'

Scott checked his watch. 'It's ten twenty-six now.'

Without another word, Jack, Scott, Emily and Drift raced out of the café. Although not before Jack had set a new world record for finishing off a plate of strawberry waffles!

The friends sped along the seafront, scattering seagulls as they went, crossed the square and hurtled through the heavy wooden double doors at the back of the village hall.

There was silence as every member of the small audience turned round in their chairs to see what the commotion was.

Don Penrose was standing behind a desk at the front, pointing at a PowerPoint slide with his pencil, explaining the difference between a common shrew and a pygmy shrew. He looked up at the noise. 'Ah, super! Our newest members have come to join our merry band.' As he stepped into the projector beam a giant shrew was displayed across his face. 'There are plenty of seats at the back.'

The friends muttered their apologies to the group and sat down. Squirming with impatience, they listened to an hour of shrew facts. At last the talk was over and everyone drifted away to the orange squash and custard creams. Scott, Emily and Jack hustled to the front and cornered Don Penrose.

'Super!' he said, smiling at them. 'You want to sign up for the Shrew Safari tonight?'

'Er, sure,' Scott said. 'But we wondered whether it might be possible to—'

'Can we see the footage from the whale-cam?' Jack butted in, cutting to the chase.

'We're really interested in it,' Emily added.

'I must say you three are the keenest new recruits we've had for a long time!' Don chuckled. 'Sure. You can view the film on my laptop while I tidy up.'

Scott ran to the desk and clicked the film open on the laptop. Jack and Emily crowded round as he began scrolling to the night of August twentieth. On the screen, a beam of light from the lamp attached to the underwater platform glowed through the murky black water like a torch through thick fog.

Small shadowy fish flickered back and forth in the cloudy glow.

'Nearly there,' Scott muttered. 'Midnight ...'

'Not much to see, I'm afraid,' Don said as he joined them.

Suddenly a large black shape shot across the screen. Scott paused the film, tracked back and zoomed in. The object was out of focus, clearly passing very close to the camera lens.

'Ah, yes,' Don sighed. 'We thought that *might* be

167

an orca at first. But it's completely the wrong shape. In fact, I'm pretty sure it's metal. Probably a piece of wreckage that's lifted off the seabed.'

'That's it!' Emily breathed.

'The Black Salamander!' Jack shouted.

'A black salamander?' Don Penrose tugged at his straggly beard. 'Oh, no, I think you'll find their natural habitat is—'

'Cheers, Don!' Jack called as the friends piled out of the hall. He popped his head back round the door and stuck his thumbs up. 'We're really enjoying the Nature Group, by the way!'

—

'So the Black Salamander passed the whale-cam, which means it must have landed somewhere near North Point,' Scott said as they sank onto a bench in the village square, shaded by a mighty horse chestnut tree studded with prickly lime-green conker cases. 'So where is it now?'

'They can't have got far without being seen,' Emily said. 'It's a pretty noticeable car!'

'Yeah, and there are some very nosy people in Castle Key. Not everyone minds their own business like we do,' Jack joked.

'You couldn't really drive out of the sea onto North Point itself,' Scott reasoned. 'It's far too steep and rocky.

What about those sand dunes nearby?'

'Good idea,' Emily said. 'We might be able to see tyre tracks in the sand . . .'

Jack jumped up from the bench. 'What are we waiting for?'

Twenty

Hidden!

The friends stood on North Point and looked down over the dunes.

Emily stared in dismay. A group of teenage boys was racing around on quad bikes. The soft sand was criss-crossed with a million fat tyre tracks.

Jack watched enviously as one of the boys stood up on his bike to negotiate the crest of a dune. He flipped it round and bounced down the other side. 'That looks fun!' he murmured. 'I wonder if they'd let me have a go.'

But Emily was furious. Those idiots had completely trashed her crime scene! She turned in a slow circle, surveying the lonely moorland. The only landmark was the old tin mine with its solitary chimney poking up into the sky. There was nothing else but some dilapidated old boat sheds at the far end of the dunes. There had once been a busy little dock there for shipping tin out to the mainland, but it had been abandoned years ago when the mine shut down.

Suddenly Emily noticed Drift trotting towards the derelict buildings. He stopped with both ears pricked up, threw back his head and howled.

'Funny!' Jack remarked. 'He was doing his wolf impression here the other night, too. I thought he was just pining for you.'

Emily shook her head. 'He does that when he can hear a high-pitched noise.'

'Looks like it's coming from near those boat sheds,' Scott said.

The friends looked at each other. None of them wanted to jinx their luck by saying it out loud, but could the unheard noise be something to do with the missing supercar?

They ran at full tilt, only slowing when they reached the old boatyard to pick their way through the nettles, docks and sea holly that sprouted through the cracked concrete. Two long-forgotten boat hulls floated like skeleton ships in a sea of weeds. It was a lonely, desolate place.

'I can hear it now!' Emily gasped. There were two noises, in fact: a soft chugging thrum and the high electrical whine that had worried Drift's sensitive ears. Both were coming from the largest of the sheds.

White paint flaked like dandruff from the crumbling bricks of the ramshackle building. It was patched up with rotting planks and the corrugated iron roof was blotched rust red, moss green and lichen yellow.

Surely nobody would hide something as valuable as the Black Salamander in this broken-down old shed, Emily thought. *It wouldn't even keep the rain out.* And yet, the weeds were flattened and there were tracks leading down the overgrown ramp to the water's edge.

'Over here!' Scott shouted. He was crouching down at the back of the shed. The chugging noise was louder here and hot air was puffing out from a pipe under a pile of bricks. 'There's a power generator in there,' Scott said. 'These are the exhaust fumes coming out.'

Meanwhile, Jack was circling the building. It should have been easy to see inside through all the gaps and cracks. But wherever he looked, his view was blocked by a metal sheet behind the broken bricks and boards. He kicked a plank in frustration. 'It's like there's a whopping great steel box inside,' he grumbled.

'That's it!' Scott cried, coming up next to him.

'Someone's using the shell of the old shed as a disguise, but there's some kind of lock-up garage inside. This must be the hiding place!'

Emily hugged Drift. 'Clever boy! You knew all along, didn't you?'

'Give me a leg-up,' Jack said, scrambling up onto Scott's shoulders. 'I might be able to see something through that big hole under the roof.'

They were all so absorbed that they didn't hear the motorboat coming into shore. Nor did they hear two men get out of the boat and walk up behind them.

But they did hear Drift's short high bark of alarm. Emily and Scott spun round.

'Whoah! Steady down there!' Jack yelled. But it was too late. Scott stumbled. Jack toppled off his shoulders and landed on his back in the weeds with a mighty *thwump!*

Jack lay with his eyes closed wondering whether he was still alive. The tingle of nettle stings on his legs convinced him that he was. He opened his eyes to see the jowly face of Frank Evans staring down at him. The forklift driver didn't look like a friendly bulldog any more. He looked like a rabid hyena ready to go for the throat.

And behind Frank Evans stood a tall fair-haired man in a polo shirt and jeans. Suddenly Jack realized that he recognized him. It was Connor Jamison!

The two men grabbed hold of the friends and

bundled them round to the front of the shed. Scott and Jack punched and kicked. Emily tried one of her kick-boxing moves. Drift nipped at ankles. But they'd been taken by surprise and there was nothing they could do.

Connor Jamison pushed aside some boards, unlocked a padlock and rolled up a shiny metal garage door. He and Frank Evans shoved the friends inside and pulled the door closed behind them.

Jack could hardly believe his eyes! The inside of the old boat shed was kitted out like a laboratory, with machines and computers and gizmos of every kind stacked round the walls. The throbbing of the generator was accompanied by the hum of the computers and the nerve-jangling whine of a drill, being operated by a man in white overalls. Bright lights had been rigged up from the ceiling, flooding the room with a harsh white glare. It was like an operating theatre. But instead of a patient wired up to all the monitors, there was a car.

The Black Salamander!

Dazzling starbursts of light reflected off its gleaming black paintwork.

A second man in white overalls was sitting in the driver's seat revving the engine.

'Go and take a break!' Frank Evans shouted. The two men in overalls stopped drilling and revving and disappeared through a door at the back. 'I told you these kids were asking too many questions,' Frank growled at Jamison.

Connor Jamison shook his head. 'We can't let them mess it up now. We're almost done!'

Jack gaped in disbelief. His hero, the cooler-than-cool Formula One driver and stuntman, was in on the plot! It was like finding out that Robin Hood had been stealing from the poor, not the rich, all along! 'I can't believe you're letting them destroy such a legendary car!' he spluttered.

Connor Jamison laughed. 'They're not *destroying* it. Just studying it.'

'Studying it?' Emily echoed.

Frank Evans smirked. 'Rizzoli Motors were *very* keen to get their hands on the top-secret underwater technology. Silverwood thought they were oh-so-clever keeping it under wraps.'

Suddenly Scott realized what was going on. It was industrial espionage! Rizzoli were one of Silverwood's main rivals in the market for cutting-edge supercars. They were stealing *information*! 'And you thought you'd help them out?' he asked Evans. 'To get your own back on Silverwood for sacking you?'

Evans' mouth twitched in surprise and anger. 'I didn't do anything wrong, but they made sure I'd never get another computer job! Serves them right!'

'And Rizzoli are paying you, no doubt,' Scott said.

Evans shrugged. 'I'm not doing this for the fun of it! The guys from Rizzoli came and talked to me as soon as I left Silverwood. They wangled me the job at Wheel

Power. We soon figured out a way to "borrow" the Salamander.'

Scott thought it best to keep Evans talking while he tried to figure a way out. 'So you took the GPS tracker to Plymouth on the lorry so everyone would think the Salamander had been shipped overseas, while Connor drove the Salamander across the channel to hide it here.'

Evans rolled his eyes. 'Monty Howard should have kept his mouth shut about that "secret" tracker of his!'

In spite of everything, Emily couldn't help feeling a twinge of triumph. She'd been right all along! 'You disabled the security alarms and drugged the guard by putting sleeping pills in the coffee from the vending machine. And you left the Wheel Power van in Plymouth earlier in the evening so you could still make your delivery to the Auto-Dynamic factory on time…'

Not to be left out, Jack joined in. 'And you used the Salamander's active camouflage to get past the cameras at the harbour!'

Connor Jamison's handsome tanned face had faded to a sickly shade of white as they spoke. 'How do you know all this?' he demanded.

'There's only one thing we *don't* know,' Scott said. 'How did you come up with *this* place?'

Frank Evans sneered. 'Rizzoli have been planning this for a long time. They kitted this place out months ago, as soon as they heard the Salamander was going to be at Wheel Power for performance testing.'

Jack glared at Jamison. 'But you were going to be a big star with the Black Salamander in the motor show and the film and everything!'

'I still am.' Jamison leaned back against the Salamander. He seemed to have pulled himself together again. 'The Rizzoli team have got all the information they need now. They took this car apart piece by piece and now they've put her back together. Nobody will know the difference when I "find" the Salamander tonight – in plenty of time for the Monaco Motor Show!'

'I suppose you'll claim the reward for finding the Salamander, too!' Scott snapped. He was starting to realize just how a clever a game Connor Jamison was playing.

'But how did you get back from the Trewidden party to steal the Salamander?' Emily asked. 'Loads of people saw you there. You were drunk.'

Connor Jamison grinned. 'It's verrrr eashy to pretend to be shloshed,' he said, slurring his words and staggering a bit. 'You just make sure you've got soda water in your champagne glass. It was everyone else who was drunk. Even Miffy didn't notice when I took her car keys out of her bag and slipped away for a couple of hours!'

'But *why* did you do it?' Jack demanded.

Jamison rubbed his thumb and fingers together. 'Rizzoli were offering a lot of money. More than Silverwood were paying me to drive the Salamander. Even the Hollywood guys are only paying me a fraction of what the leading actor gets. I have an expensive lifestyle to finance.'

Frank Evans looked at his watch. 'Enough chit-chat! We need to start getting this place cleared out. There are some ropes out the back. We'll tie these kids up.'

Jamison looked worried again. 'What are we going to do with them?'

Evans sighed. 'Well, we're not letting them go. They know far too much.'

'But if we leave them in here, they'll ...' Jamison didn't finish his sentence.

Evans replied with a chilling smile. 'Exactly. We stick to the plan. We clear this place out, and tonight we burn it down to get rid of any traces of evidence.' He shrugged. 'There may just be a few more *traces* than we expected ...'

Jamison flinched. 'But we can't—'

'Yes, we can. Kids are always messing about in old buildings,' Evans said firmly. 'Accidents happen. Now, keep an eye on them while I get some rope.'

Scott, Emily and Jack looked at each other, their eyes wide with terror. They knew they had to do something fast. If they were tied up and locked in they wouldn't get out alive.

Scott scanned the room for a way out. The door the two guys in overalls had gone through probably led to a rest area or kitchen. No escape there. But there was a smaller metal door next to it with a thick orange cable running out through a hole at the bottom. That must be where they stored the generator that provided the electricity for all the machines and lights ...

Lights! That gave Scott an idea. This place was a big metal box without a single window. If they unplugged the electricity the place would be plunged into total darkness ... but then what? They couldn't overcome Jamison, Evans and the two men in overalls by force. And if they made a run for it, Jamison or Evans could just jump in the Salamander and catch up with them. Suddenly Scott's pulse started to gallop as a truly outrageous thought began to take shape in his mind. *What if we drive the Salamander out instead?*

Scott had driven a go-kart round a track. He'd even driven a lorry to rescue Jack from the ice factory last year. But he'd never driven a supercar! He had been watching very carefully, though, when Monty Howard had shown them the controls of the Salamander at the test track. He glanced across at the supercar. It was obviously working just fine; he'd heard the engine revving only moments ago. And he was pretty sure the man in white overalls had left the key in the ignition ...

Scott took a deep breath. He could hardly believe he was contemplating such a crazy scheme, but what choice did they have?

Scott bent down and pretended to be comforting Drift. 'Jack, see that big orange cable?' he hissed through Drift's fur.

Jack gave a small nod.

'When I give the signal, you run and pull it out.'

Emily crouched next to Scott. 'It's OK, Drift, don't worry,' she said loudly. 'But won't that make all the lights go out?' she whispered.

'That's the plan,' Scott murmured. 'We're driving out of here!'

Jack faked a coughing fit. 'Are you off your head?' he hissed. 'It'll never work!'

'Are you in or not?'

Jack coughed again. 'Of course I am.'

Connor Jamison looked up from checking a text on his phone and took a step nearer.

Emily pretended to start crying. Scott put his arm round her. 'I'll jump in the Salamander,' he mumbled into her ear. 'You go to the main door and open it as soon as you hear the engine start.'

'I'll give Drift the Distraction command first,' Emily whispered under her fake sobs.

Drift wagged his tail. Distraction? His favourite command! All he had to do was cause a big commotion. And he could see just the thing! With one pounce he could knock that rack of equipment flying right on top of the horrible man coming back with a load of rope.

Emily was reaching into her bag behind her back for her torch when Jamison reached out to grab her arm. She shrank back. There was no time for torches. They would just have to operate in the dark. She looked over her shoulder to memorize the route to the door.

'Go, go, go!' Scott hissed.

'Distraction!' Emily whispered.

Drift pounced.

Jack ran.

There was an almighty crash.

Then it went dark.

Twenty-one

Nothing to It!

Jack stood with the cable in his hand blinking in the sudden darkness. He could hear thrashing about and swearing as Frank Evans tried to crawl out from under the rack of equipment. Then the whole place vibrated as a powerful engine roared to life.

He could hardly believe Scott's lunatic plan was actually working – so far!

Jack remembered where the open passenger door of

the Salamander was and felt his way in that direction. He found the opening with his outstretched hands and threw himself in.

There was a clatter of metal up ahead and a dazzling rectangle of sunlight suddenly appeared. Emily had begun to push the door up.

Jack turned to see Frank Evans lunge towards him, trailing tangled rope and shattered equipment in his wake. He kicked out and knocked Frank back as Scott jammed his foot on the accelerator.

The car shot forwards.

Just in time, Emily jumped up and gave the garage door an extra shove. The Salamander passed beneath it with millimetres to spare. Jack reached out and pulled Emily in on top of him as they sped past.

'Look out!' Jack yelled, as the Salamander began to nosedive.

Scott had forgotten that the boathouse door opened straight onto a ramp down to the sea! He pulled down hard on the steering wheel and they veered to the left, bumping off the ramp and onto the weedy concrete yard, heading towards the sand dunes.

'Where's Drift?' Emily screamed. Jack twisted round and looked back. Drift was racing along behind the car with Connor Jamison and Frank Evans close behind.

Scott slammed on the brakes.

Drift drew level with the passenger door, which was

still wide open, and leaped into Emily's arms. Jack reached round them and pulled the door closed. Scott accelerated so hard they were all pinned back against the seats. When he could move again, Jack jabbed at buttons on the dashboard, hoping he'd find something useful.

He did. A ball of green slime shot out and hit Frank Evans in the chest at point-blank range. 'Ha!' Jack yelled in triumph. 'That's for trying to squash my brother with a crate!'

Emily pressed the button again. This time a gooball splatted Connor Jamison, stopping him in his tracks. 'Bullseye!' she shouted.

'Let's try this one!' Jack laughed. He pressed another button and smoke poured out of the back of the car. The two men rolled to the side, their hands over their mouths.

Scott accelerated again and they zoomed towards the dunes. The boys on the quad bikes all cheered and raced after them. Scott was starting to enjoy himself now. This must be how James Bond felt! He skidded a turn, leaned out of the window and waved.

But suddenly something was going wrong! The car was slowing down. The engine revved and strained.

'We can't go over the dunes!' Emily shouted. 'We're getting stuck in the sand!'

Jack turned in his seat. Somehow Frank Evans had commandeered one of the quad bikes. He was racing after them, getting closer all the time.

'We'll have to go amphibious!' Jack cried.

'But I don't know how to drive underwater ...' Scott yelled.

'Don't be a wimp!' Jack yelled. 'Monty showed us all the controls when we were at Wheel Power.'

'I know, but ... it's not that simple.'

'Look!' Emily shouted. 'We're about to run out of fuel!'

Scott looked at the dashboard. It was true. The needle on the petrol gauge was pointing at Empty.

'Jack's right,' Emily said. 'We'll *have* to go into the sea. I remember Monty saying the car switches to battery operation when it dives. We won't need petrol ...'

Scott knew it was crazy but they had no choice!

He yanked the steering wheel down so hard they swirled ninety degrees in a cloud of sand. Now they were heading straight down the beach. All Scott could see through the windscreen was the blue expanse of the sea. He glanced in the rear-view mirror. Evans was standing up on the quad bike, close enough for Scott to see the splatters of green slime all over his furious face.

Scott flipped the switched marked ENGAGE UNDERWATER FUNCTION and put his foot down.

There was a whirring and clicking as the wheels

tucked in, lights and air supply came on and the shark fins popped up.

He held his breath as they plunged beneath the waves.

—

'See?' Jack laughed a few moments later. 'There's nothing to it!'

There was a strange booming feeling and the car pitched and rolled with the waves, but somehow they were cruising along under the water.

Drift didn't like it at all. He burrowed between Emily and Jack who were jammed together in the passenger seat, and waited for it to be over.

Scott studied the dashboard. He quickly figured out the display showing depth and direction. The steering wheel could now move up and down as well as left and right. He brought the Salamander up so that they were just below the surface. He remembered Monty explaining that this was necessary to put up the aerial so that the satnav and phone would work.

Emily found the special phone between the seats and called the Wheel Power test track. 'We're bringing the Black Salamander back!' she told Alesha Rahal. 'We'll be coming into shore in a few minutes.' For the first time Emily could remember, Alesha was speechless! Then she called Carrickstowe Police Station and told them there was trouble at the old boat sheds near North Point.

Scott consulted the satnav map on the computer screen on the dashboard. He had no idea how to find a good place to come ashore, but he kept an eye on the compass display. As long as they kept heading north they should hit the mainland after a mile or so. They couldn't afford to stay underwater much longer. He glanced at the air supply monitor. It was running down alarmingly fast. The system had been designed to support a single driver for twenty minutes, not three people and a madly panting dog! Scott decided not to mention it to the others. It would only make matters worse if they started to panic.

Suddenly they all pitched sideways as a massive object bumped into the side of the car. Scott's heart pounded with terror. Had they hit a boat? Now they were all thrown the other way as something just as huge buffeted them on the other side.

Jack looked out of the window.

He wished he hadn't!

A big smiling black and white face was looking straight back at him.

'K-k-k-killer whale!' he gasped.

'There's one on this side, too!' Scott cried.

Jack closed his eyes. He had never been so scared in his life. They were trapped! It was the ultimate mash-up: killer whales versus amphibious supercar. The savage force of nature versus modern technology. If this were a movie he'd pay good money to see it any day. He just didn't want to be *in* it.

Emily gave his arm a squeeze. 'They're not trying to hurt us. Orcas don't attack people. I think they're playing!' She peered out of the window. 'It's OK. They're swimming away now.'

Scott checked the direction on the satnav display. The whales had nudged the car round towards the north-west. There was a small inlet marked on the mainland coast straight ahead. With a bit of luck it was the Wheel Power harbour!

Jack wiped sweat from his forehead. 'Is it just me,' he murmured, 'or is anyone else feeling a bit woozy?'

Scott glanced at the air supply. It was on red now. 'It's just you!' he said briskly. 'Probably just the shock of seeing the whales. Nothing to worry about.' He blinked. He was starting to see flashes of colour in front of his eyes and his head was spinning …

But through it all he could just make out that the seabed was sloping upwards in front of them. The water was getting shallower.

There was a bump as the wheels hit the sand and shingle of the seabed. Scott flipped the switch marked ENGAGE LANDING FUNCTION and at last they were back on dry land, driving up onto the small beach next to the Wheel Power harbour.

Jack pushed open the sunroof and gulped down lungfuls of delicious fresh air. Emily and Drift thrust their heads out of the passenger side window. Scott rested his head on the steering wheel and heaved great sobbing breaths of relief.

'We did it!' Jack yelled as they all tumbled out.

He couldn't believe how many people had crowded onto the small beach to welcome them. Monty Howard, Alesha Rahal, Shane Hazard, Elizabeth Price and many, many more were all waving and cheering.

Shane Hazard was snapping photographs. 'If this doesn't make the front cover of *Motor Mania* I don't know what will!' he laughed.

Alesha Rahal couldn't stop smiling. 'Wow! You guys really know how to put on a good publicity stunt. This is going to be primetime and front page *everywhere*!'

When all the hugs and thanks and explanations were over, Scott, Jack, Emily and Drift stood at the water's edge and watched in silence as two curved black fins headed out of the channel towards the open sea.

Emily waved the whales goodbye.

'That was a close one!' Scott sighed.

'Good driving,' Jack said with a grin. 'Not bad for a wimp!'

Drift barked happily. He was just relieved to have all four paws on dry land again!

—

That afternoon there was such a stream of visitors at Stone Cottage that Aunt Kate had to defrost an extra batch of cakes in the microwave.

Emily and Drift were the first to arrive, of course. Detective Inspector Hassan was close behind. 'We went out to the old boat shed after you called this morning,' he told the friends, pinching the seams at the knees of his perfectly pressed trousers as he sat down. 'We caught Connor Jamison and Frank Evans dousing the place with petrol. They'd obviously decided to burn the place down to hide their tracks. They're under arrest at the police station now.' D. I. Hassan paused to take a cup of coffee and a piece of ginger cake.

'Have they told you how Rizzoli Cars paid them to steal the Black Salamander so that they could uncover all its technological secrets?' Scott asked.

D. I. Hassan stroked his moustache. 'Yes, it's clearly a case of industrial espionage. They're both refusing to talk, but we've already traced Frank Evans' connections to several of the big players at Rizzoli. And we've checked Connor Jamison's finances. He's been taking payments from Rizzoli too. He'd run up so many debts with his playboy lifestyle that I think he'd have done just about anything for the money.'

'You'll find all the details of our investigation in here,' Emily said, handing over the case report she'd spent the last two hours writing up.

Jack slid his phone across the coffee table. 'I switched to Record when we were in the boathouse. There are full confessions on here from both of them.'

The detective inspector raised his eyebrows as he took the file and the phone. 'Yes, well, thank you very much. Now, I've told you three before that you should leave police work to the professionals ...'

To the friends' relief, the lecture was interrupted by another visitor. It was Don Penrose, popping in to tell them that the two orcas had been spotted swimming out to sea along with a group of five other whales. 'Looks like they've rejoined their pod and are heading back to their migration route. Super work, everyone!' He beamed as he handed them all gold Nature Watch badges. Then he had a cup of tea and three pieces of fruitcake, before hurrying off to prepare for the evening's Nature Watch Group event.

The next visitor was Alesha Rahal. She swished in with a huge smile. 'The media are falling over themselves to get this story!' she said. '*Heroic local kids save supercar from double-crossing swindlers!* I couldn't have planned it better myself! And Monty Howard tells me that the Black Salamander is fine. No harm done. It's win-win all round!'

'But who's going to drive the Salamander for the

movie now Connor Jamison's been arrested?' Jack asked.

'Will Stone, of course!' Alesha said. 'Mmmm, this cake's good,' she murmured, biting into a slice of coffee and walnut.

Scott was puzzled. 'I thought you needed a pretty face.'

'We'll just play a different angle,' Alesha said. 'Who doesn't love "triumph over tragedy"? Now Will's got the baby too, we've got human interest by the bucketload.' She took another bite of cake. 'And there's a lot you can do with professional make-up.'

Emily grinned. 'When life gives you lemons...'

Alesha smiled. 'That's right. No one makes better lemonade than I do!' She reached into her designer handbag, pulled out an envelope and handed it to Scott.

Scott tore it open. He could hardly believe what he was seeing. 'Wow! Three VIP passes to the Monaco Motor Show,' he cried, waving the tickets in the air. 'With plane fares and everything!'

Alesha smiled. 'I've cleared it all with your Aunt Kate and Emily's parents. You'll be special guests of Silverwood Cars. Max will be there too, of course.'

If he hadn't known that Jack would tease him about it for the rest of their natural lives, Scott would have leaped across the sofa and given Alesha a hug.

Then again, Jack probably wouldn't have even

noticed. He was too busy staring at the tickets, his mouth hanging open.

Alesha stood up to leave. 'So, I guess you guys will be having a big party to celebrate tonight?'

Scott grinned. 'Actually, I just remembered something. We signed up for the Shrew Safari with the Nature Watch Group tonight.' He looked at his watch. 'It starts in half an hour.'

Jack groaned. 'Do we have to?'

'You never know,' Emily said. 'It could be the start of a whole new mystery.'

They all laughed. Emily was right. On Castle Key it really could!

Don't miss the next exciting mystery
in the *Adventure Island* series

THE MYSTERY
OF THE SECRET ROOM

Available July 2013!

Read on for a special preview
of the first chapter.

One

Great Work, Boomerang!

'*Frimbly!*' Scott snorted. 'That's not a real word!'

Jack looked down at the letter tiles he'd arranged on the board.

He should've known it was a mistake to play Scrabble with Scott and Emily. His older brother, Scott, hated to lose at anything – even though he pretended he wasn't really trying – and their friend Emily had grown up in the Bed and Breakfast run by her parents so she'd been playing Scrabble against the guests since she was a baby. Instead of *mummy* or *daddy,* her first word had probably been *quixotic* – with the X on a triple letter score! 'Of course frimbly's a real word!' he said.

'Since when?' Emily demanded.

'Since *forever!*' Jack helped himself to another of Aunt Kate's world-famous double chocolate brownies and flopped back on the sofa. 'It's from Shakespeare, actually.' If Jack had learned one thing from his English lessons at school (and to be honest, he may *only* have learned one thing) it was that, whatever the question, if you answered with *Shakespeare* you had a fighting chance of being right, or at least sounding a bit brainy. 'Methinks thou art looking a bit frimbly, good sire!' he added, to give an authentic touch.

Scott laughed so much his brownie went down the wrong way. 'What does it mean then?'

Jack gazed through the window, searching for inspiration. Unfortunately, it wasn't a very inspiring sort of day – which is why they'd ended up playing Scrabble in the first place. They'd already worked their way through Monopoly, Twister and a TV documentary about homing pigeons. Rain was bucketing against the latticed windowpanes, as if Stone Cottage were stuck inside a giant automatic car wash. Jack racked his brains for something that didn't already have a word attached to it. Luckily, making stuff up as he went along was one of his specialities. 'Frimbly?' he said. 'It's that spooky feeling when the hairs go up on the back of your neck.'

Scott threw a cushion at him. 'Yeah, right!' He yawned and stretched. 'I've had enough of Scrabble anyway.' He opened his laptop and went back to hunting zombies on his game of Total Strategy.

Emily was fed up with board games too. In fact, she was fed up full stop. It had been raining ever since they'd got back from the Monaco Motor Show a week ago – they'd been VIP guests as a reward for solving the baffling case of a disappearing supercar. After all the sunshine and celebrity, the rain-and-Monopoly combo was a bit of a let down. Worst of all, Emily thought, how were they ever going find a new investigation to work on in these conditions?

Drift and Boomerang were bored with the rain too. They were lying curled up on the hearthrug. Drift was Emily's beloved Right Hand Dog, a black, tan and white medium-sized medley of many breeds. Boomerang was Aunt Kate's new tabby kitten. Normally, Drift wouldn't be seen dead sharing rug-space with a *cat*, of course, but he made an exception for Boomerang and had called a truce.

Emily watched the rain and sighed deeply, but suddenly she jumped up from the sofa. She'd just remembered that there *was* something more exciting than another game of dominoes to look forward to: Castle Key History Week was starting tomorrow.

Emily couldn't wait! History Week only happened

every three years so she hadn't been old enough to have a proper part in it last time. This year, it was going to be about the Britons – the Celtic people of Cornwall – and their battles against the Saxons who had tried to invade from the East. Everyone on the island would be dressing up and taking part. The grand finale would be a re-enactment of the Battle of Castle Key that took place in 722 AD. 'Have you got your costumes ready for tomorrow?' she asked the boys.

Jack and Scott both groaned – but for different reasons. Jack liked the sound of the battle re-enactment. He was looking forward to charging around pretending to smite things with his choice of lethal weapon. He fancied a massive double-edged sword (he'd even chosen a name for it: The Eliminator) or a mace with brutal-looking spikes, but everything else about History Week sounded far too *educational* for his liking – especially the demonstration of clay pot making for which Emily had signed him up.

Scott, on the other hand, had only one worry, and its name was *tunic*!

The garment that the organizers had given him to wear had clearly been designed for a three-year-old.

It wasn't even long enough to call itself a mini skirt!

When Scott had tried the hideous item on last night he'd seriously considered running away from Stone Cottage to avoid having to wear it in public. Perhaps he could go and join his dad, who was away on an archaeological dig in the remote jungles of Cambodia – which is why Scott and Jack were staying with Aunt Kate for the summer. But, apart from the dreaded tunic, he loved everything about staying in Castle Key, so he'd decided against that idea. And anyway, he was fairly sure that the twelve pounds fifty he had left of his birthday money wouldn't get him to Cambodia!

Scott's contemplation of the Tunic Problem was interrupted by Boomerang suddenly leaping ninja-style across the hearth, where she began to scrabble at the base of the stone chimney breast that surrounded the fireplace. Then she crouched, staring at a crack in the stone, ears back, hackles up, stripy rump quivering – like a wild tigress preparing to pounce on an unsuspecting antelope in a jungle clearing.

Emily and Jack had noticed the strange behaviour too. 'What's Boo doing?' Emily laughed.

Jack shrugged. 'Must be a mouse behind there.'

Boomerang flicked out her razor-sharp claws from their velvety pads. Suddenly she flattened her body to the ground and shot through a tiny hole in the stonework.

Scott, Jack, Emily and Drift stared in disbelief.

A muffled mewing sound came from behind the stone.

'Oh, no!' Emily cried. 'She's stuck!'

The three friends tried calling Boomerang's name and

tempting her out with morsels of tuna and a wiggling string. Nothing worked.

'We'll have to try to make this hole bigger somehow,' Scott said.

'What with?' Jack snorted. 'You'd need a sledge-hammer to make a dent in this stuff.'

Scott sighed. Jack was right. The chimney breast had been constructed of slabs of rock so gigantic they must have been leftovers from Stonehenge. He was starting to get seriously worried now. The mewing was getting more feeble. Maybe they should call Aunt Kate from the kitchen – or the fire brigade.

Out of frustration, Scott jabbed at the gap and shoved the stone as hard as he could. To his astonishment, it moved. He pushed again. There was a grinding noise of stone against stone. The whole massive, colossal, ginormous boulder was sliding to one side.

Boomerang shot out with an indignant howl.

'Wow!' Jack breathed. 'How did you do that?'

Scott didn't answer. For one thing, he had no idea. And for another, he was too busy staring at the small chamber that had opened up behind the chimney.

'A secret room!' Emily gasped.

'More like a secret broom cupboard,' Jack pointed out. 'It's not very big.'

'What do you expect?' Scott laughed. 'A fitted kitchen and an indoor pool?' He turned back to see Boomerang sitting on the rug washing her ears. 'Great work, Boo!' he said. 'You can join our team as Chief Feline Investigator!'

Boomerang flicked her tail. Cats didn't join *teams*, they worked alone!

Emily ran to fetch her torch from her shoulder bag – she carried a full investigation kit with her at all times – and shone the beam around the little room. But there was nothing to be seen except for a small spider that scurried away into a crack. 'I bet this was a smugglers' hidey-hole,' she murmured. 'They must have stashed their loot here in the olden days.'

'Ooh, or maybe one of the Smuggling Carters hid in here,' Jack breathed, 'to escape from the tax men.'

Jack and Scott had recently discovered that they were descended from a famous family of Cornish smugglers. Jack had been obsessed with old smuggling stories ever since. He stepped inside the little room. 'Slide the stone back across,' he told Scott. 'I want to see how our ancestors felt when they were hiding.'

Scott pushed the heavy stone back into place. 'I'm leaving it open a bit,' he said. 'You might get stuck.' He grinned at Emily. 'Although it *is* tempting!'

'What's it like in there?' Emily shouted.

'Dark!' Jack called back. The voice seemed to come from the solid stone. 'I'm sure I can sense the spirit presence of one of my great-great-grandfathers. And it's dead spooky.'

'Don't you mean *frimbly*?' Scott laughed.

'Exactly!' Jack shouted. 'I told you it was a real word! Close it a bit more. I want to get the full-on smuggler-on-the-run experience!'

Scott pushed the stone until only a crack remained. 'What's the "experience" like now?' he called.

There was no reply.

Scott rolled his eyes. Jack was so predictable! No doubt he thought it would be a hilarious trick to get them all worried and then make them jump out of their skins by springing out when they pulled the stone back. Either that, or he was speechless with terror because the spider had reappeared and run up his shorts.

Scott curled his fingers into the gap and heaved the stone open again.

But Jack didn't leap out at them, because Jack wasn't there!

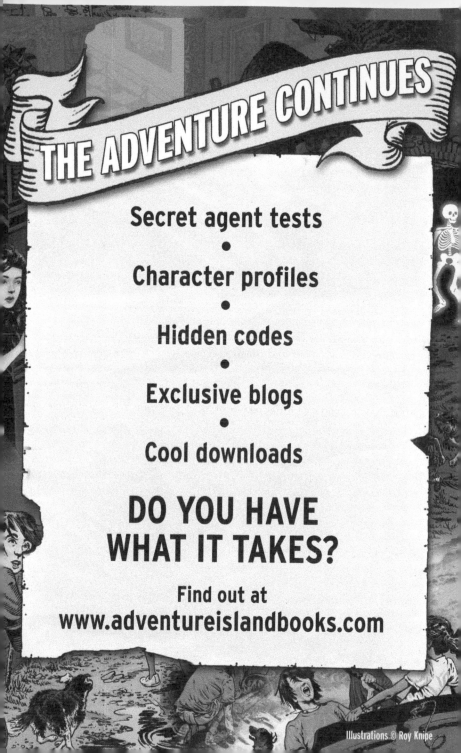

THE ADVENTURE CONTINUES

Secret agent tests
•
Character profiles
•
Hidden codes
•
Exclusive blogs
•
Cool downloads

DO YOU HAVE WHAT IT TAKES?

Find out at
www.adventureislandbooks.com